Dotted Lines

USA TODAY BESTSELLING AUTHOR
DEVNEY PERRY

DOTTED LINES

Copyright © 2020 by Devney Perry LLC

All rights reserved.

ISBN: 978-1-950692-46-0

No part of this book may be reproduced, distributed or transmitted in any form or by any means, including photocopying, recording or other electronic or mechanical methods, without the prior written permission of the author except in the case of brief quotations in a book review.

This is a work of fiction. Names, characters, places and incidents are the product of the author's imagination or are used fictitiously. Any resemblance to actual events, locales or persons, living or dead, is coincidental.

Editing & Proofreading:

Elizabeth Nover, Razor Sharp Editing

Julie Deaton, Deaton Author Services

Karen Lawson, The Proof is in the Reading

Judy Zweifel, Judy's Proofreading

Cover:

Sarah Hansen © Okay Creations

OTHER TITLES

The Edens Series

Indigo Ridge

Juniper Hill

Garnet Flats

Jasper Vale

Crimson River

Sable Peak

Christmas in Quincy - Prequel

The Edens: A Legacy Short Story

Haven River Ranch Series

Crossroads

Sunlight

Treasure State Wildcats Series

Coach

Blitz

Rally

Clifton Forge Series

Steel King

Riven Knight

Stone Princess

Noble Prince

Fallen Jester

Tin Queen

Calamity Montana Series

The Bribe

The Bluff

The Brazen

The Bully

The Brawl

The Brood

Jamison Valley Series

The Coppersmith Farmhouse

The Clover Chapel

The Lucky Heart

The Outpost

The Bitterroot Inn

The Candle Palace

Maysen Jar Series

The Birthday List

Letters to Molly

The Dandelion Diary

Lark Cove Series

Tattered

Timid

Tragic

Tinsel

Timeless

Runaway Series

Runaway Road

Wild Highway

Quarter Miles

Forsaken Trail

Dotted Lines

Holiday Brothers Series

The Naughty, The Nice and The Nanny

Three Bells, Two Bows and One Brother's Best Friend

A Partridge and a Pregnancy

Standalones

Clarence Manor

Rifts and Refrains

A Little Too Wild

CHAPTER ONE

CLARA

"What are the yellow lines for?"

"They're dotted lines," I answered.

"But they aren't dots." August sent me his famous look through the rearview mirror. The look that said I was wrong, and he was skeptical of everything I'd taught him in the five, nearly six, years of his life. He'd picked up that suspicion toward the end of his kindergarten year, and I'd been getting the look a lot this summer.

"No, they aren't dots. But when you go fast enough, they sort of look like dots."

"Why aren't they called stripes?"

"I think some people might call them striped lines."

"That's what I'm calling them." He dipped his chin in a single, committed nod. Decision made. "What do they mean?"

"It means that if you get behind someone going slower

than you, and as long as there isn't someone else coming in the opposite direction and the road is clear, you can pass the slower driver."

August let my explanation sink in, and when he didn't ask another follow-up question, I knew I'd satisfied his curiosity. For one topic.

One. Two. Three.

"Mom?"

I smiled. "Yes."

"How much does the ocean weigh?"

Now there was a whopper. But my son's endless questions never disappointed to entertain. I'd lost count of how many topics we'd covered on this trip alone. August was nothing if not inquisitive. I couldn't wait to see what he'd do with all the facts he was storing in his head for later.

"With or without the whales?" I asked.

"With the whales."

"With or without the yellow fish?"

"With them."

"And the blue fish?"

"Yes. All the fish."

"Even the starfish?"

"Mom," he groaned. "How much?"

I laughed, glancing at the backseat, then turned back to the road. "The ocean, with the whales and the fish and the starfish, weighs more than the moon and less than Jupiter."

His little forehead furrowed as he rolled that one around. "That's a lot."

"It sure is." My cheeks pinched from smiling, but that was the case with August. When he was younger, I'd told him he had magical powers. That if he smiled, I smiled. Every time. That was his magic, and he used it often.

I adjusted my grip on the steering wheel as the tires whirred over the pavement. The Cadillac floated down the road more than it rolled. In a way, it was like we were flying, skimming just above the asphalt as we soared toward California.

August stared out his window, his legs kicking. He was already restless to get out of the car even though we'd just started today's journey, navigating the roads of Phoenix as we headed toward the interstate.

We were halfway through our two-day journey from our home in Welcome, Arizona, to Elyria, California.

In total, the trip was only eight hours, but I'd split it up, not wanting to torture my son with an entire day strapped in a car seat. Last night, we'd stopped in Phoenix and had a nice evening at the hotel. August had spent the hours after dinner doing enough cannon balls into the pool to sink a pirate ship. Then he'd passed out beside me in bed while I'd read a book for a few hours of distraction.

This morning, after a continental breakfast of pastries and juice, we'd loaded up the Cadillac and hit the road.

"Mom?"

"August?"

"Do you like this car?"

"I love this car," I answered without hesitation. Even though I hadn't spent enough hours behind the wheel to consider it mine, I loved this car. For reasons that would be lost on my son.

"But there's no movie player," he argued. It was the third time he'd reminded me that the Cadillac didn't have a video console like my Volkswagen Atlas.

"Remember what I told you. This car is a classic."

He huffed and sank deeper into his car seat, totally unimpressed. "How much longer?"

"We've got a while." I stretched a hand to the backseat, palm up.

He might not be having the time of his life in the car, but he was still my best pal. With a crack, he slapped his hand to mine for a high-five.

"Love you, Gus."

"Love you too."

I returned my hand to the wheel and relaxed into the buttery leather seat.

Yes, I loved this car, even if it wasn't mine to keep. The 1964 Cadillac DeVille had once been a heap of rust and dented metal. The car had rested on flat tires in a junkyard in Temecula, California, home to bugs. Probably a mouse. And two runaway teens.

The on-ramp for the interstate approached and I took it, my heart galloping as I pressed the accelerator.

Today was the day. Today I was returning this

Cadillac to one of those runaway teens. Today, after more than a decade away, I was going to see Karson.

My stomach twisted. If not for my firm grip on the wheel, my hands would shake. Twelve, almost thirteen years ago, I'd left California. I'd left the junkyard that six of us had called home for a time.

My twin sister—Aria—and me.

Londyn, Gemma and Katherine.

And Karson.

He'd been our protector. The one to make us laugh. The shoulder to cry on. He'd made a bad situation bearable. An adventure. We'd survived the junkyard because of Karson.

And the Cadillac was his, a gift from Londyn. I was simply the delivery girl.

In another lifetime, Londyn and Karson had made this Cadillac their home, back in the days when it didn't have glossy, cherry-red paint or a working engine. But Londyn had hauled the Cadillac out of the junkyard and had it completely restored. She'd kept it herself for a time, then set out to give it to Karson.

Her trip from Boston to California had only made it to West Virginia. From there, Gemma had taken the Cadillac to Montana. Katherine had been the third behind the wheel, driving it to Aria in Oregon. Then my sister had brought it to me in Arizona.

Ready or not, it was time to finish what Londyn had

started. I'd put off this trip long enough. But it was time to make the handoff, to take the last leg of the journey.

The final trip.

It wasn't the hours on the highway or the destination that had kept my heart racing since we'd left home yesterday. It was the man waiting, unsuspecting, at the end of the road.

Had Karson found whatever it was he'd been searching for? Had he built a good life? Was he happy? Did he remember our moments together in vivid clarity like I did? Did he replay them during the long nights when sleep was lost?

Will he recognize me?

"Mom?"

I shook off the anxiety. "Yeah?"

"How much longer till we get there? Exactly?"

"About four and a half hours."

He groaned and flopped his back. "That's gonna take *forever*."

"You could take a nap. That will make the trip go by faster."

August sat up straight and sent me a look of pure poison through the mirror. "It's morning."

I pulled in my lips to hide my smile. "How about some music?"

"Can I play a game on your phone?"

"Sure." I rifled through my purse in the passenger seat, finding my phone. Then I handed it back to him.

August unlocked the screen with the code, though his face worked at times too.

I'd be forever grateful to Devan, August's father, for helping me create this magnificent boy. But I was also forever grateful that August looked exactly like me. He had my blond hair, though his had been lightened by the Arizona summer sun, whereas I got mine highlighted at the salon. We shared the same nose and the same brown eyes. August's second toe was longer than his big toe, something he'd also inherited from me.

He was mine.

Mine alone. The lawyer I'd hired when August was a newborn had assured me that once Devan had signed his rights away, Gus was mine.

It wasn't the life I'd wanted for my son, to grow up without a father, but it was better this way. Devan hadn't wanted a child and no amount of coercion would have turned him into a decent parent.

So I showered my son with love and attention. I would, shamelessly, for the rest of his life.

Good luck to any girlfriend he brought home. Fathers were allowed to put boyfriends through an interrogation. Well, this mother was taking that liberty too.

The sound of a math game drifted through the cab as August played on my phone. The dings and chimes of the app mixed with the hum from the wheels on the road.

And I breathed as the miles toward California whipped by.

It was only a state. Only a name. But somewhere along the way after we'd left Temecula, California had become synonymous with the past.

California meant hungry days. California meant dark nights. California meant death.

It was the reason Aria wouldn't go back. Same with Katherine. Neither of them had any desire to set foot in California again. Maybe, if I'd begged, Aria would have come with me, but I wouldn't have asked that from her. Besides, she'd just had a baby and was in no shape for a road trip.

Aria and Brody were currently enduring the sleepless, grueling nights as parents of a newborn. Logistically, it made sense for me to take this trip now. Brody was both brother-in-law and boss, so while he was taking time to spend with Aria and the baby, there was a lull in work to do as his assistant. With August on summer break from school, this was the window.

Or maybe I knew that if I kept avoiding the trip, I'd never take it.

I could do this.

I have to do this.

Because for twelve years, I'd been holding on to a hope. A distant hope, but one powerful enough that it had kept me from letting go and moving forward.

It was time.

After only thirty minutes, August gave up on his math game. He asked me another long string of questions, and then by some miracle, he fell asleep. Swimming at the hotel last night must have worn him out.

He was drooped in his chair, his head hanging down at an angle that would have given me a neck kink, when we approached the California border. Elyria sat on the coast, north of San Diego, and we still had hours to drive, but crossing the border was a hurdle of its own.

I'd opted for a southern route through Arizona, wanting to avoid Los Angeles traffic. And Temecula.

Visiting California was enough for one weekend. Returning to the town where we'd spent our childhood was an entirely different matter. Temecula had happy memories from the early years, from the happy lives Aria and I had lived before our parents had been killed in a car accident when we were ten. After that, I could count the number of happy memories on one hand. Temecula was full of ghosts, and though they still called to me at times, I wouldn't go there even with August as my steadfast companion.

This trip was about closure. It was about Karson. That was plenty.

I gripped the wheel, my heart in my throat, as I passed the sign at the state border. *California*.

My stomach rolled and sweat beaded at my temple. I sucked in a long breath, dragging it through my nose to then push out my mouth. *In and out. In and out, Clara.* Just like Karson had taught me years ago when he'd witnessed one of my panic attacks.

I hadn't had one in years.

My hands were trembling when my phone rang. I stretched for it in the passenger seat, checking that August was still asleep. It always amazed me that he could sleep through about anything.

"Hey," I answered, not at all surprised that my sister was calling. Whether it was a twin thing or a sister thing, we usually had a good pulse on each other's moods, even thousands of miles apart.

"Hi." Aria yawned. "Are you okay?"

"No," I admitted. "This is harder than I thought it would be."

"Are you in California?"

"Yes." I blew out a trembling breath. "I can do this, right?"

"You can do this. You're the bravest person I know."

"No, you are."

Aria had brought us both through the hardest time in our lives. While I'd fallen apart after our parents' deaths, she'd kept us moving. Ten-year-old me had gone comatose for a few weeks, mostly from the shock. What kid wouldn't buckle under that much heartbreak? *Aria.* Maybe it was because I'd needed her and she'd stayed strong. She'd kept me going through the motions until the fog of grief had cleared.

Then I'd vowed never to fall apart again. As a child, I'd made good on that promise to myself. As an adult and parent, failing was not an option.

Aria thought I could make this trip and she was right. I could do this.

Granted, she didn't know what had happened with Karson. Maybe if she knew the truth, she would have given me different advice.

"How are you doing? How's Trace?" I asked, needing a different topic to focus on.

"We're both good." There was a smile in her voice and a tiny squeak hit my ear. "He's nursing. I think he likes his name."

"Because it's perfect." Broderick Carmichael the Third. *Trace.* It had taken them over five days to give the baby a name, but when I'd called to check in last night from the hotel, Aria and Brody had proudly announced Trace.

"How is the drive?" Aria asked.

"It's fine. Taking *forever* according to August."

Aria laughed and yawned again.

"I'll let you go. Take a nap if you can, okay?"

"That's the plan. Brody fell asleep about an hour ago. Once he wakes up, we're switching."

I was glad she had him. I was glad he had her.

Maybe it had been watching my sister fall in love with my friend that had been the final push to send me on this trip. Someday, maybe, I wanted love. I wanted a man to hold me at night. I wanted a man who'd be a good role model to August. I wanted a man who made me feel cherished.

Until I confronted the past, I'd always wonder. I'd always compare.

I'd always think of Karson.

"Call me when you get there," Aria said.

"I will."

"Take a picture of Karson with the car if you can. I think Londyn would like to see that."

"Good idea. I think she would too," I said. "Love you."

"Love you. Bye."

When I ended the call, the anxiety from earlier had lessened. That was the way with my sister. On a bad day, we had each other. It had been that way our entire lives.

There was a good chance—better than good—that I'd return home with a bit of a bruised heart. And she'd be there to help it heal.

I can do this.

There was no turning back now. The Cadillac had sat in my garage for too long as it was. Maybe it would have been easier if not for the track record with these handoffs. For every trip this Cadillac had taken, one of my friends had found love.

Londyn had met Brooks in West Virginia, thanks to a flat tire.

Gemma had returned to Montana and found Easton waiting.

Katherine and Cash had fallen in love on the sleepy highways between Montana and Oregon.

Aria had come to Arizona and realized the hate she'd harbored for Brody had actually been affection.

I had no delusions that this trip would result in a major life change. I fully expected to be the one woman who returned home single. Months of preparing myself for that reality hadn't made it easier to swallow.

Yet there was that glimmer of hope I'd buried deep. It mingled with the fear because, unlike my friends, I hadn't set out into the unknown unsuspecting.

I knew exactly who I was seeking.

Had his smile changed? Did he grin like he used to? God, I hoped so.

I hoped that whatever had happened to Karson in the past twelve years, his smile hadn't dulled. Because on my darkest nights, when the ghosts escaped their confines at the California border and drifted into Arizona, it was the memory of Karson's smile that chased them away.

That, and my son.

August stirred, blinking heavy eyelids as he came awake.

"Hey, bud."

"Are we there yet?"

I gave him a sad smile. "No, not yet. But we're getting closer."

He sagged in his seat, his eyes still sleepy and his cheeks flushed. "Mommy?"

"Yeah?" My heart squeezed each time he slipped and called me Mommy. One of his friends at school last year had told August that he called his mom *Mom* and not *Mommy*. From that day forward, I'd been Mom except for the rare moments when he was still my baby boy.

"Do you think we can go swimming as soon as we get there?" he asked.

"Probably not right away," I said. "First we need to stop by my friend's house. Remember?"

"Oh, yeah. Is it going to take a long time?"

"No, not too long."

"Then we can see the ocean, right?"

"Yes, then we'll see the ocean."

August yawned but sat straighter. His eyes lost their sleepy haze and his gaze flicked out his window, chasing the sage brush and sand that bordered the interstate. "What do you think is more scary, a shark or a lion?"

This boy would never know how grateful I was for his questions. He'd never know that he kept me grounded. He kept me sane. He kept me going. "That depends. Is it a hammerhead shark or a tiger shark?"

"Hammerhead."

"A lion."

He nodded. "Me too."

The questions continued until the open road clogged with vehicles and the Cadillac was swallowed up in traffic. August was about to come out of his skin by the time we made it to the outskirts of San Diego.

We stopped for lunch and August devoured a well-earned Happy Meal at McDonald's. Then after a refill at a gas station, we loaded up once more for the drive along the coast. After we passed the city, the Sunday traffic moved in the opposite direction, most people returning home after a weekend trip.

Thirty miles outside of Elyria, the ocean came into view, and I decided to pop off the interstate for a quieter highway that hugged the coast. August's eyes were wide as he stared at blue water and the waves glittering under the bright July sun.

"Let's do something fun," I told August, touching the brake to ease us into a turnout along the road.

"What?" He bounced in his chair, then his jaw dropped when I moved to put the convertible top down. "Cool!"

We both laughed as I pulled onto the road. August's hands shot into the air, his hair, in need of a cut, tousling in the salt-tinged wind.

He needed sunscreen. He should be wearing sunglasses. But for thirty miles, fun was more important than being the responsible mother every moment of every day. That and I didn't want to do anything to ruin that smile on his face.

I needed that smile as the nerves crept in, twisting up my insides and making it hard to breathe. So I braced my knee against the wheel and raised my arms. "Woohoo!"

"Woohoo!" August cheered with me.

His laughter was the balm to my soul, and I soaked it in, reminding myself that this was August's trip too. This was his summer vacation to the ocean, something he could brag about on his first day of first grade this fall.

Vacation. We'd explore the oceanside. We'd shop for souvenirs we didn't need and eat too much ice cream. We'd have a fun trip, then go home. Brody had volunteered his jet to save August from a two-day return trip in a rental car.

The speed limit dropped as we passed a sign welcoming us to Elyria.

I gulped.

My phone chimed with directions through town toward the address I'd entered days ago. Brightly colored shops lined the main road. A couple crossed the road ahead, each carrying surf boards. Signs for parking areas sprang up every few blocks, directing people toward the beach.

Later I'd explore this charming town, but at the moment I kept my focus forward, listening intently to the navigation. When I turned down a side street, I was so anxious I didn't bother taking in the neighborhood around us.

Then we were there. Karson's address. The destination was on our left.

I slowed the Cadillac to a crawl in front of a white stucco house with arched windows and a terra-cotta roof. The tiled walkway to the front door was the same rich, caramel brown as the clay. Two baby palm trees towered over the green yard, and off to the side of the house was a garage.

I pulled around the corner, parking in the driveway. The thunder of my heart was so loud I barely registered August's question.

"Mom, is this it?"

I managed a nod as I turned off the car and unbuckled my seat belt. Then I stared at the house. How would I make it to the front door? Maybe I should have called first. Karson might not even be home. If not, I guess we'd come back later.

But this was definitely his house. I double-checked the number beside the garage door.

"Can I get out?" August asked, already unbuckling his harness.

"Sure." I'd need him with me for this.

I climbed out of the car, walking on unsteady legs to his side to help him out. Then with my son's hand in mine, I stood in the driveway and let the sun warm my face. The sound of the ocean was a gentle whisper on the air. The scent of salt and sea hit my nose.

Aria had lived on the Oregon coast for years, and though the smell was similar, there was something sweeter in the Elyria air.

Karson had always said he wanted to be close to the ocean. He'd wanted to learn how to surf. I was glad he'd gotten that wish.

The sound of a door opening caught my attention and I turned, just in time to watch a tall man with dark hair step outside. A short-trimmed beard shaded his sculpted jaw. He was wearing a pair of khaki cargo shorts slung low on his narrow hips. His green T-shirt stretched over his broad chest and clung to the strength in his biceps. His feet were bare.

Karson.

My heart skipped.

He'd grown up. Gone were the lanky arms and legs. Gone was the shaggy hair in need of a cut. Gone was the youth from his face.

This was Karson Avery, a man who stole my breath. But he'd done that at nineteen too.

Those beautiful hazel eyes studied me, then darted to the car as he came toward us. A crease formed between his eyebrows as he took it in. Then they moved to me and that crease deepened.

My stomach did a cartwheel. *Please recognize me.*

If he didn't . . . I clung to August's hand, drawing strength from his fingers. It would break my heart if Karson had forgotten me. Because in all these years, he'd never been far from my mind.

Karson's feet stopped abruptly and his entire body froze. Then he blinked and shook his head. "Clara?"

Oh, thank God. I swallowed the lump in my throat. "Hi, Karson."

"I can't believe it." He shook his head again, then his gaze shifted to August. "Hi there."

August clutched me tighter and murmured, "Hi."

"Is it really you?"

"It's me."

"It's really you." A slow smile spread across his face, wider and wider.

It hadn't changed. There, on the face of a man, was the smile from the boy I'd loved.

The boy I'd loved before his life had gone one direction and mine had gone the other.

And between us streaked those dotted lines.

CHAPTER TWO

CLARA

Twelve years earlier...

"Here." Aria tossed me the dry-erase marker.

I caught it and rubbed my fist on the van's wall, erasing yesterday's number. Then, popping the cap, I wrote today's number in blue. The sharp scent of the marker had become the smell of hope.

Sixty-one.

We had sixty-one days until our eighteenth birthday. Sixty-one days until we could leave the junkyard as legal adults and get on with our lives. After three years of living in this van without electricity or heat or air conditioning, our time here was coming to a close.

I'd thought as the days had ticked away, I'd be more excited to say goodbye to this shitty old van. I guess leaving any home was hard, even a dirty one. Even my uncle's.

Though any shithole was better than living under that bastard's roof.

"Are you sure you don't want to go to Montana?" Aria asked from her bedroll where she was bent, tying her shoes.

The laces had been white at one point, just like the laces on mine. But after nearly three years, they were permanently a brownish red—the color of the dirt outside that we did our best to keep from tracking in.

"I don't know." I shrugged. "That's where Londyn, Gemma and Katherine went."

"Exactly my point."

"Don't you think we should, like, find our own place?"

"Yeah," she muttered. "I guess so. Then where?"

"LA?"

"Hell to the no." She stood up and plucked her favorite black hoodie from the backpack that was her closet. "I want out of California. Forever."

"I just want out of this freaking town." I took one long look at the number on the metal wall, then recapped the marker and tossed it into my wooden crate.

Sixty-one.

The excitement would come. Eventually. Right?

"Will you water my plants for me today?" Aria asked.

"Sure." I had nothing else to do.

On the days when I wasn't working, life in the junkyard was boring. The day would stretch without TV or a phone or . . . anything. So I'd water her plants. I'd sweep out the van with the handheld broom I'd gotten from the dollar store a couple years ago. Both chores would take an hour total. Then I'd have to find something else to do.

"What do you want me to bring you back from the restaurant?" she asked.

"Food."

My answer was the same as always. Just like Aria's answer on the days when she was stuck here and I went to work at a truck-stop diner. I washed dishes for six dollars an hour. It was below minimum wage but since the owner paid me in cash under the table and didn't ask questions about why I hadn't been in school all last year, it was worth the cut.

Staying off the grid was the only way we'd made this living arrangement work.

For sixty-one more days, Clara Saint-James was a ghost.

Then Aria and I would leave here and rejoin society with a real address and social security numbers and birth certificates—the documents tucked away beneath my bedroll in a plastic bag. We'd made sure to take them from our uncle before we'd run away.

Maybe when we got out of here, we'd actually get driver's licenses. A credit card. A bank account.

"Any requests?" Aria asked. She worked as a dishwasher too at a greasy spoon about a thirty-minute walk from here. The owner of her restaurant had actually asked for an application.

Aria had listed me as her mother's name, the junkyard as our address. Thankfully, they hadn't tried to call the fake phone number she'd put on the application. Or if they had, they hadn't asked why the call hadn't gone through.

Like me, she was paid under the table, so why her boss had needed an application, I wasn't sure. Whatever the reason, all that mattered was that we both worked in restaurants. The food was worth more than the hourly wage.

On the days we worked, neither of us had to worry about a meal. And normally, there'd be enough left in the kitchen for an extra sandwich or two to bring home.

"Ham and cheese," I said. It was Karson's favorite, not that I'd tell Aria that was the reason I always asked for it.

"'Kay. I'm out." She stood at the mouth of the van, waiting.

I walked over and wrapped my arms around her.

The night our parents had died, I hadn't wanted to give my mom or dad a hug good night. I'd been in the middle of a game of Fallout on my PlayStation. I'd gotten to level eight and the blocks had been falling so fast. My fingers had flown over the control. And when my parents had kissed me goodbye, when they'd told me to have fun and be good for our babysitter, I'd dismissed them with a grunt.

Hours later, on their way home, a drunk driver had crossed the center line and crashed into their car.

Ten-year-old me hadn't understood that life was short.

I'd been so worried about a stupid video game that I hadn't hugged my parents goodbye.

I wouldn't make that mistake again.

"Be careful." I let Aria go and watched as she hopped out of the van.

When her shoes hit the dirt, she looked up at me and waved. "Bye. Have a good day."

"You too."

I didn't like the days when we walked into town alone. Yes, we'd been doing it for nearly three years, but that didn't mean it was safe. Until we were gone, until we left Temecula and turned eighteen, we would never be safe. Not until we had control over our own lives.

Aria didn't head for the small gate in the junkyard fence that served as our own personal door. Instead, she rushed over to Lou's shop, disappearing into the bathroom.

I stayed standing at the end of the van, waiting until she came out. Then with another wave, she disappeared through the rusted cars and stacks of metal parts.

I sighed, scanning my rust-colored world. Everything here was tinged orange-brown. Some of the old cars still had flecks of paint—teal or black or red. This van had once been white. But with every passing day, the colors disintegrated, little by little. Chip by chip. It was a losing battle against the wind and the sun and the rain and the dust.

The only bright, fresh color came from Aria's plants. She'd been growing more and more this year, ever since the girls had left.

I think she missed Londyn and Gemma and Katherine more than I did. Not that I didn't miss them. I did. I missed our friends. It was just . . . easier with them gone.

I didn't have to work so hard to hide my crush on Karson.

Instead of masking it from five people, I only had to hide my true feelings from two—my sister and Karson himself.

Easy when I was here alone.

The sun would be warm today, perfect for growing, so I hopped down from the truck and found the old coffee can that Aria used to water her plants. It rested by one of the truck's flat wheels.

Our home wasn't fancy but it kept the rain out, mostly. And the mice. It was an old delivery vehicle, the back a rectangular metal box. It had gotten into an accident at some point, hence its lifetime membership in this graveyard with the other broken-down heaps.

The front end was smashed. The hood was a crumpled piece of metal, and wherever the engine was, I doubted it had survived. But the box was mostly solid. The few jagged holes in the metal siding let in some natural light. We'd covered them with plastic shower curtains to keep out the wind and water and bugs.

It was time to replace the curtains. They were tinged with dirt and film. But with only sixty-one days to go, I didn't see the point in wasting the money.

Inside the truck, Aria had her side and I had mine. At

the foot of each of our bedrolls rested our backpacks. By my pillow, I kept neat stacks of tattered romance novels I'd bought for a dime at the thrift store. Most I'd read ten or eleven times.

The books formed a little shelf of sorts to hold a bottle of water, a flashlight and my battery-powered alarm clock. At night, that shelf also held the foldable knife I'd stolen from Uncle Craig.

I patted it in my pocket, feeling its weight against my hip. That knife went with me everywhere, even in the junkyard.

Taking the can, I walked toward the shop. It was one of two buildings in the junkyard, the other a shack where the owner, Lou Miley, lived.

Lou's windows were arguably dirtier than my windows, but at night, they let out enough of a glow that we knew Lou was inside. In the winter, a steady plume of smoke would stream from his metal chimney and the scent of a campfire would fill the air. Lou was a recluse most days. He'd venture outside only when necessary to run the yard.

I cast a quick glance at his shack, sniffing bacon in the air. The kitchen window was cracked and Lou must have had a nice breakfast.

My stomach growled. The granola bar I'd scarfed earlier would have to do until Aria came home from work. We needed to get to the grocery store and pick up some more bread and peanut butter, but I didn't get paid until

Friday.

And I refused to raid our savings.

Alongside the plastic bag of legal documents under my bedroll was another full of cash. Half of everything Aria and I made went into that pouch. It was our future, and we'd built it with sheer determination and discipline.

We were saving up to get out of here. That money was going to be the foundation for the days when we could afford bacon for breakfast.

And a stove.

And a refrigerator.

Shoving the hunger aside, I walked to the shop. It stood nearly three times as tall as Lou's shack, tall enough that all of his equipment could fit inside.

I slipped in through the metal side door and flicked on the row of lights. The smell of grease and oil and gasoline hit my nose as I weaved past the machinery. An excavator with a claw on its arm. A tractor with a large bucket. A forklift crowding the doorway to the shop's bathroom.

The florescent light above the cracked mirror flickered, giving me an instant headache. I went to the deep white sink, stained from years of dirty hands and not enough bleach, and twisted on the faucet to fill the can.

It might not be the biggest or brightest bathroom, but it was better than nothing. And we'd cleaned it enough that I didn't have any issue walking around in my bare feet.

Lou allowed us to use this bathroom. It still smelled like Aria's shampoo and conditioner from her morning shower. The floral scent clung to the air and I breathed it in as the can filled.

The shower stall was just large enough to stand in and wash under the silver head. There wasn't even a curtain to separate it from the rest of the bathroom. But a shower every day made this place livable. It kept the dirt from building up. It kept my honey-blond hair from hanging limp to my waist.

Most days, I braided it to keep it out of my face, but at night, when I lay down on my pillow, it was a comfort to know that at least my hair was clean.

With the can filled, I left the bathroom, shutting off the light behind me. Then I retreated through the shop toward the door, only to have it whip open just as I reached for the handle.

Water sloshed out of the watering can, soaking the toes of my shoes.

"Shit. Sorry." Karson stepped back, holding the door for me. "I didn't know you were in there."

"That's okay." My heart raced and my voice was breathy. Because, holy abs, he was shirtless.

No shirt. None. I was staring at a bare chest, naked arms and a fantastic belly button, which wasn't actually all that interesting, but beneath it a line of dark hair disappeared beneath the gray towel wrapped around his waist. The whole image was . . . *wow*.

Don't stare. Don't stare.

My mantra this year.

I dropped my gaze, pretending to inspect my wet shoe.

This wasn't entirely new. I'd seen Karson without a shirt on before, but it hadn't been for a while. And back then, he'd belonged to Londyn. It had been easier to pretend I wasn't head over heels for the guy when his girlfriend had always been nearby.

Now it was impossible.

He was lean, we were all lean, but Karson was cut too. His chest was broad, his stomach hard and flat. There was a V just where the terry cloth circled his hips.

My mouth went dry thinking about the slight bulge beneath that towel. The flush in my cheeks felt hot and red.

Oh my God. I sucked at this. How was I supposed to hide my crush on Karson when he walked around in nothing but a towel?

"I . . ." I swallowed hard and stepped through the open door, moving past him, careful to keep a wide berth. "I'll get out of your way."

"You're not in my way."

I gave him a small smile, then dropped my chin to my chest and watched every one of my steps as I scurried away, only daring to look back when I heard the shop door close.

"Ugh," I groaned, looking up to the blue sky. "What is wrong with me?"

Karson was never going to like me. Ever. He was in love with Londyn. The two of them had lived together in the Cadillac for years. She might have left for Montana with Gemma and Katherine, but that didn't mean Karson would ever want me instead.

Londyn, with her silky blond hair three shades lighter than my own. Londyn, with her pretty smile and rich green eyes. Karson and Londyn. He loved her. He'd had sex with her. I'd heard them once, giggling and kissing. Then the Cadillac had started to rock, and I'd had to sleep with the pillow over my face to block out the noise and hide my tears from Aria.

He wanted Londyn, not me.

The only reason Karson was still here at the junkyard was because he saw Aria and me as little sisters. He'd stayed to watch out for us even though he'd just turned nineteen and by all rights should have left over a year ago.

Like Londyn, Gemma and Katherine.

The girls had done exactly what Aria and I would be doing in sixty-one days. The day they were all eighteen, they'd hopped on a bus destined for Montana. Katherine had found them housekeeping jobs at a resort or ranch or something.

But Karson had stayed, saying it wasn't safe for Aria and me to be here alone.

He wasn't wrong.

It would just be easier if I didn't have this epic, ridiculous crush on a guy who was never, ever, ever going to like me. Karson probably thought I was a freak. As the months went on, it got harder and harder to make eye contact as we talked. Then there were the times that I stuttered like a moron. Example: today.

"Great, Clara. Just great," I huffed as I reached the truck and Aria's plants.

Whereas I'd spent my extra change on books, Aria had splurged on a hand trowel and seed packets. How she got anything to grow in the dry, hard-packed dirt of the junkyard was a mystery, but the greenery proved it possible.

She'd planted cosmos and morning glories. She had Shasta daisies and sweet potato vines. I'd water them all, grateful for their color to brighten our temporary home.

The watering can was empty too soon, and I'd need to take a few more trips to the bathroom for refills, but I climbed into the truck instead. Once Karson was showered and dressed, I'd venture out. In the meantime, I'd spend my morning studying.

And do my best to forget about the definition in Karson's arms and the gold and green sparkle in his hazel eyes.

I kicked off my shoes, leaving them by the sliding door we left up most days to let in the fresh air. Then I made myself comfortable on my bedroll, which was just a sleeping bag that had lost most of its fluff over the years. It was still warm, combined with the fleece blanket I draped on top, but even the foam cushion under the covers didn't hide the fact that we were sleeping on a metal floor.

My GED study guide rested on top of the wheel well.

I grabbed it, cracking it to the section where I'd left off last, and began hammering through practice questions.

I was in the middle of a language arts section when a knock came on the wall.

"Hey." Karson vaulted into the truck, fully clothed.

I forced a smile to hide my disappointment.

"Brought you a banana," he said. "I just bought a bunch yesterday. Thought you might want one."

"Thanks." I took it as he handed it over.

"You're welcome." He sat down across from me on Aria's bed, his long legs eating up the floor space between us. "How's studying going?"

"Okay." I ran my hand over the guidebook's page.

Karson had gotten me this book. I'd told him that I wanted to get my GED after we left the junkyard and two days later, he'd brought this home. It was new, unlike the used books I could afford. The cover was glossy. The page corners were crisp and square, meaning it hadn't been cheap.

We spent our money on necessities. Food. Clothing. Blankets. Toiletries. Not GED study guides.

I knew he'd stolen it. He hadn't admitted it, but there'd been no receipt and it hadn't come in a plastic sack. It wasn't the first time he'd stolen, and I doubted it would be the last. I'd never forget the first time I'd watched him palm an apple from the grocery store and start eating it in the aisles. He'd dropped the core into a garbage can before we'd gone through checkout, no one the wiser.

Sure, it bugged me a little. Aria and I didn't steal. There was a pinprick of guilt when I cracked the book's pages, but it was also a gift. A gift from Karson for my future. I'd been so touched by his thoughtfulness that I'd cried after he'd dropped it off—that was before I'd realized it had likely been shoplifted.

We all did what we had to do.

I shut the book and ripped open the banana's peel. I was hungry and wouldn't turn down food, but someday, I would never eat a banana again. The same was true for granola bars and canned green beans. Peanut butter and honey sandwiches too.

When Londyn had lived here, she'd worked at a pizza place. It was the only thing we'd eaten a lot of that I hadn't completely lost the taste for. Though I never craved it.

"What are you doing today?" I asked as I chewed.

"Nothing. I'm bored. Are you working?"

"Nope." I took another bite and almost gagged. Freaking bananas. I hadn't liked them before coming here either.

"Want to play cards?" he asked.

I shrugged, trying to hide my excitement at time alone with Karson. "Sure."

An hour later, we'd moved from my place to his, and I was kicking his ass at gin rummy. "Gin."

"Gah." He tossed his cards onto the discard pile. "We need a new game."

I giggled and collected the deck. The edges were worn

and gray. The nine of clubs had a noticeable bend. "Poker?"

"Yeah." He stood and disappeared into the other section of the tent, returning with a little cup of toothpicks. We didn't have money to gamble or actual poker chips, but toothpicks worked fine.

After Gemma and Katherine had left, their tent slash fort had been unoccupied. The structure was a collection of metal sheets and tarps that Gemma had engineered into a shelter.

For a guy who stood over six feet tall, it made sense for Karson to get out of the cramped backseat of the Cadillac. He'd moved in here, taking up Gemma's old room. The common area had lost some of its life without the girls here. Katherine's tiny paintings on the wall weren't as bright as they used to be.

"What do you think will happen to this place when we all leave?" I asked Karson, shuffling the cards.

He resumed his seat across from me, leaning against one of the makeshift walls. "I don't know. Probably nothing, knowing Lou."

Lou had sectioned off the junkyard. His house, the shop and the area where we lived was off-limits to customers. Whether it had always been like that I wasn't sure, but from the time Karson had come here, Lou had all but given us free rein of our small portion of the yard.

Beyond his shack swam a sea of rusted cars and old parts. People would come in during the day and rummage through the piles. Lou would emerge to show them around, always careful to keep them away from our area.

"What do you think will happen to Lou?"

Karson lifted a shoulder. "I don't know that either."

"Will you come back here? After you leave?"

"Maybe. You?"

"Maybe." *Maybe not.*

Karson pulled a toothpick from the cup and rolled it between his fingers. The movement was mesmerizing, much like his face. He'd shaved today. The dark stubble that matched the color of his hair was gone from his cheeks and jaw. It made his lips seem softer. His smile wider.

I caught myself staring and tore my eyes away to focus on the cards. "Five-card draw? Or hold 'em?"

"Hold 'em."

We used to have poker tournaments in this room, when the girls were here. "Do you miss them? Londyn and Gemma and Katherine."

"Sure." He counted toothpicks, handing me a handful of twenty. "Don't you?"

"Yeah, I do." I didn't miss seeing him kiss Londyn, but otherwise, yes.

They were my friends. Londyn was the reason we'd found the junkyard in the first place. We'd lived in the same trailer park and after she'd run away from her junkie parents, we'd tracked her down. A couple of the kids who'd worked with her at a pizza parlor had known that she'd been hanging out at the junkyard during the day, ditching school. Though they hadn't known she'd been living here too.

"Do you think we'll ever see them again?" I asked.

"Honestly? No." He looked up and the gentle smile he gave me nearly broke my heart. "I mean, maybe someday. But I doubt it."

"Even Londyn?" The question slipped out before I could swallow the words. I knew they'd broken up. Clean. As friends. But maybe he hoped to see her again one day. Maybe he'd continue on to Montana when our sixty-one days were up.

"Yeah. Londyn too." Karson gave me another smile. One that made me want to scream. It wasn't his playful smirk or his wide grin when he thought something was funny. It was the sweet smile, for a little sister.

Kill me now.

I dealt the cards and focused on the game, winning the first five hands in a row. When Karson was down to three toothpicks, he went all in on a bluff. I called it.

Game over.

"Damn." He laughed. "Not my day for cards. Let's do something else."

"Okay. What?"

"Feel like going for a walk? I wouldn't mind stretching my legs."

I pushed up off the ground, brushing off my jeans. Then I followed him outside and through the junkyard, toward the ten-foot chain-link fence that had a row of barbed wire on top.

Lou didn't like people in his space. He'd erected the fence to keep them out.

We were the exception.

The main entrance had two large gates set on wheels. Lou kept a chain and padlock around them unless he was expecting a customer. The PRIVATE PROPERTY sign hung below another that read MUST CALL FIRST.

But there was another entrance, a small gate that was hidden from the road and bordered by an old car. Karson had discovered it his first night at the junkyard years ago. To anyone passing by, it looked blocked. But the gate opened enough for us to squeeze in and out. Some days, we strolled through the main entrance if Lou had gotten up and unchained the lock. But mostly, we used the side gate.

Once on the road to town, we settled into an easy pace on the asphalt. There were no sidewalks bordering the one-mile stretch of pavement. Or what we assumed was one mile. None of us knew for sure, but before Karson had dropped out of school and run away, he'd been able to run a mile in under six minutes. One day, bored, he'd run the road as a test.

The junkyard was on the outskirts of Temecula, lending it privacy. The closest neighbor was halfway down the road and even then, the overgrown trees and tall fence hid the house and its occupants from view. Or maybe . . .

"Do you think they planted all the trees in an attempt to block out the junkyard?" I asked Karson as we walked past the house.

He chuckled. "Definitely. Wouldn't you?"

"Totally." I laughed. "So where are we going?"

"Where do you want to go?"

Anywhere with you. "I don't care. I'm up for whatever."

"How about the movie theater?"

"Last time we tried to sneak in we got caught. And you got into a fight."

"That guy was a fucking asshole, Clara. He shouldn't have grabbed you like that."

It hadn't been a big deal. The theater manager had taken my arm and pulled me toward the exit. He'd literally been trying to throw me out.

Except the moment he'd touched me, Karson had exploded. He'd punched the manager so fast I'd barely registered his fist flying through the air before the loud crack of knuckles hitting jawbone.

As the manager had collapsed onto the floor, another employee, a tall, lanky kid, had rushed Karson. Those two had shoved and grappled and traded a couple of hits until Karson had landed another solid punch to the nose—I'd never seen a nose gush so much blood. But it had been enough for us to get away before the cops had shown up.

Karson's eye had been bruised for a couple of days. It wasn't the first black eye he'd gotten, and again, I doubted it would be the last. I worried most about the fights he got into when none of us were there to drag him home.

He protected us. But who protected him?

"We'll go to another theater," he said.

"That's a long walk."

"We've got nothing else to do. Besides . . ." Karson reached into his pocket and pulled out a wad of cash. "This time we'll pay."

"No, don't waste it." I pushed at his arm, urging him to put the cash away. I didn't want to risk anyone seeing it and coming after him. Not that there was anyone around to see. The two of us were alone on the road.

"It's settled. We'll go to a movie. And I'll have the prettiest girl in the universe in the seat beside me."

I blushed and elbowed him in the ribs. "Flirt."

"With you? Always."

If only that flirting meant something.

It was pointless to argue—and I really wanted to see a movie—so I let Karson treat me to an afternoon of fun. Of normalcy.

In a dark theater, we weren't a couple of runaway teens who ate popcorn by the fistful because at our home there was no such thing as a microwave. Or asked for extra ice in our shared Coke because both ice and Coke were scarcities.

We were just Karson and Clara. A hot guy. And the girl who wished he saw her as more than a friend.

Still, by the time we left the theater, my smile felt permanent.

We talked about the movie the entire way home, our favorite lines and the twist at the end that Karson had seen coming but I hadn't. Evening was upon us by the time the junkyard came into view, which was good since I liked to be back by dark. So did Aria. Unless it was absolutely necessary, we didn't take late shifts and were home before sunset.

"That was fun," Karson said as we walked through the gate.

"Thank you." I smiled up at him and soaked in that handsome face. The strong jaw. The straight nose. The high cheekbones. In my romance novels, the heroes always had those traits, and Karson was most definitely my kind of hero.

"Thanks for hanging with me today." He nudged his arm against mine, escorting me to the truck. "Even if I let you win at cards."

"Whatever." I swatted him back.

He chuckled.

The noise must have drawn Aria's attention because she poked her head out of the truck. "There you are. You didn't leave a note."

"Shoot. Sorry." I winced. We always left notes if our plans changed. It wasn't like we could text on our nonexistent phones.

"You suck. I was worried." Then she disappeared, probably sulking on her bed.

"Oops." Guilt hit hard. Aria was my number one. I should have remembered a note. "I'm a bad sister."

"No, you're not." Karson put his hand on my shoulder. "Better go apologize."

"Yeah." I took a step away but stopped and turned back. "Thank you."

"You already said that."

"I know." My cheeks blushed as he stared at me so intently, as if waiting on my every word. If only that were the case. "Sweet dreams, Karson."

"Then I'll have to dream of you."

I rolled my eyes, covering up the fact that a cheesy line sent a swarm of butterflies fluttering in my belly. "Flirt."

He winked. "With you? Always."

CHAPTER THREE

CLARA

"Forty-seven," Aria said as she wrote it on the wall.

That should have been cause for celebration. We were only forty-seven days from freedom. Why the freaking hell wasn't I more excited? I mean . . . there was a little bit of anticipation. A lot of nerves. And mostly dread that seemed to grow faster than Aria's plants as the number ticked lower.

Because in forty-seven days, Karson would be a memory.

He didn't think we'd ever see the girls again, and what scared me the most was that he didn't seem to mind never seeing three people that we'd lived and survived alongside. When Aria and I left, would he feel the same?

He'd stayed here for us. He clearly cared, right? Maybe we were different. Maybe . . .

"I was thinking of asking Karson to go with us." I

blurted the thought that had been in the back of my mind for two weeks. "Wherever we go. If you don't care. I just don't want him to be alone."

"That's cool. I don't think he will, but I don't care if you ask." Aria put the marker away and scooped her hair into a ponytail.

Even though my sister and I were fraternal twins, we had similar features. Our mouths. Our noses. Our brown eyes. And our hair.

Or . . . we used to have the same hair.

Aria had come home with a dye box from the grocery store yesterday. Every week we kept five dollars out of our pay to use on whatever our hearts desired. Mine was normally spent on books or a tabloid magazine—another attempt to be like normal girls my age and fawn over the latest Hollywood heartthrob. Aria had spent hers this week to become a brunette.

"It's going to take me a while to get used to seeing you with brown hair."

She smiled and stroked her chocolate strands. "Me too. But I love it."

If I ever dyed my hair, I was going lighter. Like Londyn. I wanted hair like sunshine.

"Okay." She sighed, letting her shoulders sag. "We'd better go."

I stood from my bedroll and followed her out of the truck. We were both working today and even though my shift started an hour after hers did, we were walking into town together. Then she would come to the diner and hang out until I was finished so we could walk home.

The two of us had just started down the path toward the gate when the creak of hinges echoed across the junkyard from Lou's shack.

Aria and I both looked over as he shuffled out, heading for the fence with a ring of keys in one hand.

We slowed, waiting and watching, as Lou unlocked the padlock on the chain wrapped around the fence's posts. He hadn't noticed us yet. Or maybe he had but was just ignoring us. When it came to Lou, I wasn't sure how much attention he paid to his teenage squatters.

Lou was wearing a white T-shirt, the cotton thin and dingy. Like everything around here, dirt had become a part of its fibers. Aria and I didn't own a light color, not anymore. Anything we'd brought with us that had been white or a pale shade had been ruined early on. Even with a weekly trip to the laundromat, it was simply too hard to keep whites bright.

Lou's jeans bagged and sagged on his frame, the faded red suspenders he wore at all times the only thing keeping them up. He was a big man, taller even than Karson.

He would have been a mountain if he had stood straight and pulled his shoulders back. As it was, they were always hunched and curled forward. The gray scruff on Lou's face covered his jaw. The white hair on his head was oily and stuck up in all directions.

Lou finished with the padlock and shoved the fence

open a few feet. Then he turned and trudged back to his shack, not sparing us a glance.

"See?" Aria shot me a smirk as she continued on to the fence. "Told you he loves us."

"Maybe he has a customer coming."

"He totally opened the gate for us so we didn't have to squeeze through the little one today. Because he loves us."

I laughed. "You're delusional."

"You know I'm right."

Aria wanted to believe there was an adult in this world who looked out for us. Maybe she was right and Lou did care. Part of me wanted to believe it too because we'd never really know.

Lou had hardly spoken to us in years and with just weeks left to go, I doubted we'd ever know the man. Not one of us had set foot inside his shack, even Karson.

Following Aria through the gate, I cast a backward glance over my shoulder to Karson's tent, but there was no sign of him. I hadn't seen him in two days.

That time seemed precious now.

I just hoped he hadn't gotten into any trouble.

"How about Florida?" Aria asked as we started down the road toward town.

"Too far away."

"But it's so green and there's the ocean. I think I'd like the ocean."

"It's on the exact opposite side of the country. Traveling that far is going to cost too much. Besides, if you want the ocean, we can just find another place in California."

"No. Never. I want out of here." She spoke in a way that said she wouldn't be back either.

"Um . . . how about Vegas?" I held my breath, hoping she didn't immediately nix the other idea I'd been toying with lately.

Aria looked at me like I'd grown another arm. "Seriously?"

"It's not that far away. There are tons of hotels where we could work as housekeepers or whatever. And there's money there, Aria. It's *Vegas*."

"True," she muttered, thinking it over for a few moments. "I guess if we didn't like it, we could leave."

"Exactly." A rush of excitement swelled, exactly what I'd been searching for.

We walked a few more steps until she nodded and said, "Okay. Vegas."

I smiled and did a fist pump with the hand she couldn't see. I'd thought it would take more convincing. One of the line cooks at the diner had visited Vegas a couple of weeks ago and had told me he was getting ready to move there. He'd spent an entire shift telling me about the Strip and the hotels and how he'd already lined up another job.

The way he'd described the neon lights of the casinos had been so vivid that I'd wanted to see them for myself. There was no way I'd go without Aria. Since I'd convinced her so easily, maybe I could convince Karson too.

He wasn't set on a certain place, at least not one that he'd told me about. So why not Vegas? The three of us could find a place to rent, an actual apartment with a roof and bedrooms and a bathroom.

Hope for that future blossomed as we walked. Visions of a living room filled with Aria's plants and a TV for Karson to watch swirled in my mind. Maybe one day, Karson would be watching a movie on that TV and I'd be curled into his side on the couch that we'd picked out together.

"What the hell?" Aria whispered.

"What?"

"Her." She nodded down the road where a woman was jogging our way.

Any normal kid might not wonder about a woman running on a quiet road, but Aria and I were far from normal.

"Have you ever seen her before?" I asked.

"No. You?"

"Never." In the nearly three years we'd been living in the junkyard, not once had we encountered a jogger or pedestrian of any sort on this road. Not once. People didn't walk around here. And there were many, many roads to run on that were better than ours.

One neighbor, farthest from the junkyard, had five pit bulls. They were contained by the thick fence that surrounded their property, but those dogs loved to bark. The ruckus they could create still startled me at times.

Then there was the neighbor who'd planted the jungle to block out the world. Because the trees and shrubs were so overgrown, walking past the mouth of their driveway was borderline creepy, so we always walked on the opposite side of the street.

The junkyard itself had enough KEEP OUT signs to shingle a mansion's roof.

Nothing about this road was welcoming. It screamed *go away*. And this woman running did not belong.

Her dark hair was trapped under a headband that was as electric blue as her leggings. The white of her shirt was nearly blinding under the morning sun. Her fuchsia shoes crunched on the rocks that littered the pavement. Not even the city's street sweepers came this way.

She was too clean. Too colorful. Too happy.

"Morning." The woman smiled and waved as she passed us.

Aria and I didn't respond. We stared at her, our necks twisting to keep her in view as she jogged on by.

"Think she's lost?" I asked.

"I don't know," Aria muttered, her legs moving faster. "It's weird, right? Or am I just getting paranoid?"

"Then I'm paranoid too."

Maybe other seventeen-year-old kids didn't get gut feelings, but my sister and I had learned a long time ago to trust our instincts.

"Maybe she just got turned around," Aria said. "One jog down our road and she'll never be back."

"Yeah."

On cue, the dogs started howling and snapping at the chain link. Aria and I both paused enough to glance back.

The woman yelped and leapt away from the fence. Her hand pressed against her heart. Yet she didn't turn back. She kept on running, getting closer and closer to the junkyard with each step.

"Come on." I took Aria's arm. "You'll be late."

She checked her black wristwatch, one that matched mine. "What are you going to do before your shift?"

"I'm going to hit the store. Get some bread and maybe applesauce or something. We're almost out of peanut butter too."

"We need cat food."

"Okay."

When Katherine had lived with us, she'd adopted this stray cat. The beast was unfriendly to everyone but her, but when she'd left, she'd begged us to keep feeding it. So Aria and I bought the damn thing food, feeding it enough to survive but not so much that it would lose the incentive to hunt mice.

We reached the edge of town and walked past two industrial buildings, then turned down the block that would lead us to an arterial. When we got to the first stoplight, I hugged her goodbye. "Have fun at work."

"You too. See you later."

She went one way and I went the other, making my way the seven blocks to the closest grocery store. My shopping didn't take long. I didn't have the money to fill a cart or the means to get it home, so I picked out the few items on my list, made it through checkout and found a bench outside to load my haul into my backpack.

I was just zipping it up when a flash of electric blue caught my eye.

The jogger.

I stood straight and faced her.

She was staring at me, hovering beside the store's brick wall. Her face wasn't red. Her chest was dry, not even a sheen of sweat above her breasts. No way this lady had gone for a strenuous run.

The hairs on the nape of my neck stood on end. With a fast swoop, I swung my bag over a shoulder and scurried away, dodging the few people going in and coming out of the grocery store.

I didn't look back to see if she'd followed as I hurried to the diner, where I ducked in the rear employee entrance and let the door shut with a slam.

"Hey." One of the cooks spotted me as he came out of the walk-in refrigerator.

"Hey." I forced a shaky smile, hovering by the door until he left. Then, when I was alone, I cracked the door open and scanned the alley. The dumpster was overflowing and due to be picked up today. The cars parked next to the building all belonged to the staff.

Besides a crow pecking at a clump of dry grass, the alley was devoid of any life. No lady in electric blue.

"You're early."

I jumped at my boss's voice and let the door close again, turning to face her. "Yes, ma'am."

"Dishes are waiting."

I nodded and got to work, stowing my backpack in a small cubby. Then I tied on a grease-stained apron and took my place at the restaurant-grade dishwasher, spending my day scrubbing away syrup and ketchup from thick, heavy ceramic plates.

When Aria arrived an hour before my shift ended, she poked her head in to say hello before retreating into the diner to wait at a small table and drink a Dr. Pepper. The waitresses were supposed to charge for soda and refills, but they never made Aria pay.

The hour she waited was the longest of the day. All I wanted to do was tell her about the creeptastic jogger, and by the time my shift ended, the nervous energy was making my bones rattle. The second we stepped outside, I told her the whole story.

"Do you think she's a cop?" I asked. "Like, maybe undercover or something. Or a private investigator? Maybe the sick fucker hired her to find us."

The sick fucker. Our uncle. Aria and I referred to him with a variety of expletives, only speaking his name when necessary.

"Do you think he's been looking all this time?"

"I don't know." The worry on her face made the knot in my stomach bunch tighter. "He's crazy."

And after all he'd done—to us, to her—there was no telling how psycho he'd gone after we'd run away. "Let's just . . . get home."

Home to the junkyard, where there was a padlock to keep people out. Where there was a maze of scrap metal and broken cars to hide in.

Where there was Karson.

We walked so fast that both Aria and I were panting as we squeezed through the side gate. Between the two of us, we'd kept a constant eye behind us. There'd been no sight of the woman in blue in town, and when we'd hit the road to the junkyard, there'd been no sign of anyone. Even the dogs were absent, probably down for an afternoon nap or snack inside with their owners.

"Tomorrow, we should go in even earlier. Like, mix up our routine," Aria said as we unloaded our things into the truck.

"Yeah. Good idea. And maybe we don't walk home right after work. We could go to a park or something."

She nodded and kicked off her shoes. Then she plucked my newest book off the stack. "Can I read this?"

"Sure. I'm going to go say hi to Karson. Tell him about the jogger."

"'Kay." Aria settled on her bed and opened the book to the first page.

She'd be lost in the first chapter before I returned. It

was a really good book, maybe good enough to make the take-to-Vegas pile.

I'd take them all if weight and space were unlimited, but I had to pack my entire life's possessions into bags I could carry. Everything else in the truck would be left behind, because when we left here, I was beginning to realize, we wouldn't be coming back.

Climbing down from the back of the truck, I made my way to Karson's tent. When I passed Londyn's Cadillac, I ran a hand over the top. A twinge of longing and guilt made me pull my hand away. Londyn had been my friend and I had a major crush on her boyfriend—ex-boyfriend.

Not that it mattered. Karson didn't like me that way.

When I reached the tent, I drew in a steadying breath. *Be cool. Don't smile too much. Don't stare. Just be cool.* Then I rapped my knuckles on the metal siding beside the tarp that was the door.

"Karson?" I called when he didn't answer.

A groan caught my ear. I hesitated, waiting, then peeled away the tarp to poke my head inside. "Karson?"

"Yeah," he grunted from his bedroom.

"Are you okay?" I dropped my gaze to my feet. He was a boy—man. My mind immediately went to Karson naked and . . . doing things. To himself.

Freaking romance novels.

"Can I come in?" I asked, squeezing my eyes shut to block out the image of a naked Karson.

"Yeah."

I shoved the tarp aside and stepped inside, giving myself a minute to adjust to the dim light. He was lying on his sleeping bag in the fetal position. "Oh my God. Are you sick?"

He hummed his agreement.

I rushed to his side and pressed a palm over his forehead. "You're burning up."

"I'll be okay. Just need to rest."

No. This was bad. It was rare that any of us got sick, but it was terrifying when we did. There were no moms here who knew what to do. No doctors to call and ask for advice.

I shoved off the floor and raced out of the tent, running to the truck. "Aria, Karson's sick."

"What?" She flew off her bed, the book tossed aside as I vaulted inside.

"Where's the first aid kit?" I asked even though I was already rushing for the backpack where we kept the small plastic box.

Gemma had gotten sick a couple years ago. It had scared Karson enough that he'd gone to Lou, who'd given him a bottle of Tylenol. After Gemma had left for Montana, the medicine had been given to us in case of emergency.

Today was that emergency.

I ripped the first aid kit open and grabbed the Tylenol, then scanned the truck for the fresh bottle of water I'd bought at the store earlier. From my clean clothes stack, I plucked the last washcloth. Aria and I were planning to go to the laundromat tomorrow so I could wash the others.

"I'm going to stay with him," I said, jumping down to the dirt.

"Want me to come too?"

I shook my head. "We can't all get sick."

She sighed, crossing her arms. "I hate this."

"Me too. Lock yourself in tonight. I'll sleep in the tent."

"Be careful. Yell if you need me."

"I will." I rushed back to Karson, finding him exactly where I'd left him.

His entire body was trembling and his face ashen.

"Here." I cracked the water bottle, then popped the lid on the medicine. "Can you sit up?"

It took him a moment, but he opened his eyes and shoved up on an elbow to take the pills from my hand and chase them down with a sip of water.

"More." I tipped the bottle back to his lips.

He shook his head.

"More," I insisted and only when he swallowed a long gulp did I let him lie back down. I dumped some of the water onto the washcloth. It wasn't cold, but it was cool. Then I laid it across his brow.

"Thanks," he murmured and opened his eyes to scan the space. "Where's my blanket?"

"Here." It was tucked against the wall beside his feet. I grabbed it and shook it out, making sure there wasn't a spider or another bug between the folds. Then I laid it over Karson, watching as he clutched it to his heart.

I sat back, watching. Was the Tylenol working? What if it didn't? "I think I should get Lou."

"No." Karson reached for me and took my hand, tucking it to his chin.

The whiskers on his jaw tickled my knuckles, but even past them, his skin felt too warm. "Karson, I should get Lou."

"I'll be okay. Just . . . sit with me."

"Okay," I agreed, but if he didn't stop shivering soon, I was getting Lou.

I inched closer, crisscrossing my legs. Then I slipped my hand free of his and pulled the cloth from his forehead, folding and refolding it so it would feel cool.

"Lou gave me this blanket. Did I tell you that?" Karson's eyes drifted shut. His words were hushed and slurred.

"Yeah."

We all knew this blanket was special.

Maybe Aria was right after all and Lou did love us.

After Karson ran away from home, he'd wandered around Temecula for a while. Somehow, he'd chanced upon the road to the junkyard, hoping to find a spot to sleep, like on a bench or under a tree.

He'd come toward the junkyard and spotted a fire. Lou had been burning wood scraps in a metal barrel. Or maybe it had been trash. Lou burned most of his garbage, even though Karson had told me it was illegal. Lou just put wood on top to hide the garbage.

The light from the fire had caught Karson's attention, illuminating the side gate. After Lou had gone inside, Karson had shoved it open and snuck in. Then he'd camped out on an old truck's bench seat in the yard.

He kept coming back for a month, nearly every night.

"Scared me to death," Karson murmured. "That night he came out with the blanket. I thought I was so clever, coming in and out under his notice. Then he tossed the blanket on me, and I realized he'd known all along."

I gave him a sad smile. "Aria thinks he loves us."

"He does. In his own way." Karson's shivering became violent. Sweat sheened his cheeks and his breaths were coming in shaky pants.

"Karson, I think—"

"Stay. I'm fine. Don't leave, Clara. Promise."

Ugh. This was stupid, but that didn't stop me from whispering, "Promise."

And I stayed. All night. Until dawn cracked the horizon and the sun's rays bled through the gaps in the tent's walls. Until Karson's fever broke.

I stayed until he opened his eyes and smiled. "I had the sweetest dream."

"About what?"

"You."

I sighed, relief coursing through my veins. He was okay.

"Flirt."

CHAPTER FOUR

CLARA

"Clara." A hand touched my shoulder, shaking me awake.

I flinched, sitting up on my bed in a jolt. My fingers scrambled for the knife by my side and I gripped the hilt, ready to slash and cut.

"Whoa." Karson held up his hands and backed away. "Clara, it's me."

"Oh." My heart climbed back down my throat and I blinked rapidly, clearing the sleep haze. "Sorry."

"You sleep with a knife?" His gaze darted between my face and the weapon.

I shrugged as embarrassment crept into my cheeks. God, I'd almost slashed at Karson. *Smooth, Clara.* "It's, um, just in case, you know?"

A crease formed between his eyes. "Yeah."

I shoved the hair off my forehead and slumped against

the truck's wall. It was bright out and the heat was beginning to seep inside like it did every afternoon. My midmorning nap must have lasted longer than I'd planned.

"Are you feeling okay?" Karson asked.

"Yeah." I yawned. Staying up beside him while he'd sweated through his fever had worn me out. "Just tired."

"Thanks. For last night."

"Sure." I shrugged. "How are you feeling?"

"Better. I was just getting ready to head into work. My shift starts at two."

"Are you sure you should be working?"

"I'll be fine. It's only for a few hours to cover for one of the guys until close."

He didn't look fine. His skin was pale, and his hazel eyes were missing their usual mischievous glint. Whatever bug he'd caught had wiped him out.

Karson needed to rest, but instead, he'd walk to town and go to the car wash. There was no such thing as a sick day in our life. We worked rain or shine.

So this afternoon he'd run the sprayer for any of the vehicles that came through, and by the time he was done, his jeans would be nearly soaked. Karson always joked that he didn't need to do laundry, even though he still took his clothes to the laundromat anyway. In this heat, those jeans would be dry, though stiff, by the time he made it back.

"I'll come to town with you." I shifted and picked up my shoes that I'd kicked off earlier.

"You don't have to."

I smiled. "I don't have anything else to do today. Besides, it'll be unbearable in here soon."

By early evening, the truck would be sweltering. I tucked my knife into my jeans pocket, then slipped on a shoe. When I looked up, Karson's eyes were on the pocket.

"You sleep with it."

I dropped my gaze. "Yeah."

"How long?"

"Always." Since we'd run away. Aria had stolen one from our uncle too.

We'd added the knives to our collection of backpacks and flashlights and raincoats. We hadn't stolen those from our uncle, though we certainly had stolen the money to buy them with. When we'd dragged our haul to the cash register at the sporting goods store and handed over a fistful of cash, the clerk had looked at us funny.

But since Craig had stolen everything from us, everything from our parents, that money had been ours to spend.

"Ready?" I asked Karson when my other shoe was on.

Karson nodded, but he didn't move from the floor. "Do you, um . . . the knife. Is it because of Lou? Or . . . me?"

"What? No! Of course not." I hated that he'd think I was scared of him. Or Lou.

"Then why?"

In the years that we'd lived here, I'd never shared the

nasty details about why we'd left our uncle's. Aria and I had skimmed over the real story.

We'd told Karson and the girls that our parents had died in a car accident. We'd told them that we'd been sent to live with our uncle. And we'd told them that he'd been a bastard who'd made living under his roof impossible, so we'd run away.

End of story.

None of them had asked questions because they'd all had their own stories. Their own skeletons and demons.

The only ones who'd realized that Uncle Craig had been a pervert were Londyn and Gemma.

Londyn, because she'd lived two trailers down from ours and had seen Craig around. And Gemma, from her one trip to the trailer park with my sister.

Aria had decided to go back and rescue my bike. She'd wanted to surprise me—or she'd known I would have said hell no—so instead of taking me, she'd taken Gemma.

Uncle Craig had been there, though he hadn't seen them. But Gemma had spotted Craig. When she'd told me about the bike fiasco, she'd shivered and commented how his beady eyes had freaked her out.

I had nightmares about those beady eyes.

So did Aria.

That was the extent of what we'd shared. After the bike, which was parked beside a pile of junk because it had two flat tires we couldn't afford to fix, Aria and I hadn't returned to our former neighborhood.

Our friends here had no idea that Craig used to watch us in our sleep. That three times I'd come out of the shower to find him in the bathroom, waiting with my towel pressed to his nose.

Craig was the reason we carried the knives. Because if he ever found our junkyard home, I'd kill him before living under his roof again.

"Just . . . in case," I told Karson. Maybe someday I'd tell him more, but today was not that day.

"All right." He pushed up to his feet and led the way outside.

I closed the sliding door on the truck, bathing my belongings in darkness. With the door closed, it would be stuffy, but I'd take some stale air over a swarm of bugs.

"Short shift today, huh?" I asked as I followed Karson out of the yard for the street.

"Yeah. One of the guys needed to leave early. A doctor's appointment for his kid or something. So I said I'd come in and take the rest of his shift. It's money."

We didn't turn down money.

After Karson's eighteenth birthday, he'd gone to his boss at the car wash and told him he was going to find a better-paying job. To Karson's surprise, his boss had asked him to stay and given him a raise.

He was a real employee now, with a job application and tax withholdings. Karson had even gone to a local bank and opened a checking account, using the junkyard's address as his own. Whenever Lou got the mail, anything addressed to us kids was left in the shop's bathroom for us to find.

I hoped that once Karson built up a little in his checking account, he'd stop stealing.

"Have you and Aria decided where you'll go?" Karson asked as we set out down the road.

I nodded. "We were actually thinking Las Vegas."

"Sin City. I like it."

He liked it? Really? *Ask. Just ask.* I took a deep breath, listening to our footsteps on the pavement. "Would you, um . . . would you want to come with us? Because that would be cool. If you want."

"Thanks, but actually, I think I'm going to explore for a while."

No. My heart crashed to the street, splattering blood over my dirty shoes. But I forced a smile. "E-exploring sounds fun. Are you going to Montana?"

Would he go after Londyn? Did he still love her? I couldn't blame him if he did. Londyn was amazing and smart and funny and sweet. Of course he loved her. We all loved her.

"Nah." Karson shook his head. "I think I'll head toward the coast. I'd like to hit the ocean, breathe some clean air for a while. Learn to surf."

Part of me was overjoyed that he wasn't chasing his ex. The other part was still devastated because I would lose him soon.

"The ocean sounds fun," I lied. The ocean sounded

lame and not nearly as fun as Las Vegas. I still had forty-six days. Maybe I could change his mind. "Don't get eaten by a shark."

Karson chuckled. "I'll do my best."

"Maybe you can come and visit us. In Vegas."

He looked down and grinned. It was a grin that made my insides go fuzzy and the heart that had fallen only a minute ago do a tiny flip. "I'd like that."

I smiled. "Me too."

He stared at my mouth for a moment and the crease between his eyebrows came back.

"What?"

"Nothing." He shook his head and faced forward. "So what are you going to do while I'm at work?"

"Maybe go to the library. Or the thrift store."

"Getting another one of your books?" He nudged his elbow with mine. "A little Fabio action?"

"Whatever." I bumped his arm with my shoulder. "You just wish you looked like Fabio."

"Fabio wishes he looked like me." Karson pretended to flick his hair. The dark locks had grown longer this year. It had been a while since he'd gone to get it cut. It curled at the nape of his neck and bangs draped over his forehead.

Last night, when he'd been asleep, temptation and concern had gotten the best of me, and I'd run my hands through his hair. It was as silky and soft as I'd expected.

Lucky for me, Karson would never know. That touch,

along with my epic crush, would be my secret. Not even Aria knew how I felt about Karson.

It was probably for the best that we were going our separate ways, right? *Ugh. No.*

I mean . . . we'd have a lot to do in Vegas. Karson sort of distracted me. Without him around, I'd probably stay more focused.

Aria and I would need to find a place to live. We'd need to get jobs. As soon as I could get signed up for the test, I was going to earn my GED. I didn't need a boyfriend distracting me from building a life. It was almost time to become an adult, right?

Ugh. No, again. Having Karson with us would just make it all better.

"Want to hear something strange?" I asked, ready for a new topic.

"Duh."

"Yesterday, Aria and I saw this lady jogging toward the junkyard."

"Jogging?"

"Yup. Seriously, have you ever seen a jogger on this road?"

"No. Never."

"Strange, right?"

Karson nodded. "Yeah."

"Oh, it gets worse. Aria and I split up at the stoplight so she could go to work. I went to the store to get a few things and I was outside, packing up my bag, and the jogger was there. She was, like, watching me."

Karson slowed his steps and his forehead furrowed. "Are you sure?"

I nodded. "For sure. I think she followed me."

"Have you ever seen her before?"

"No. Neither had Aria."

He frowned and glanced around, but as usual, we were alone on the road. "Could just be a coincidence."

"Maybe. Probably."

"Keep an eye out. Watch for her."

"Aria and I thought we should mix up our schedule a little. She left for work earlier this morning than normal. I'll do the same tomorrow when I go in."

"We should all start walking together. I'll come in with you both. Even on the days when I'm not working."

"You don't have to do that."

He winked. "I want to."

God, it was hot when he winked. He had this sexy grin afterward that made me want to melt. "Thanks." I bit my lower lip to hide a goofy smile.

"Always." He slung a hand around my shoulders and pulled me into a sideways hug.

I tensed, unsure of what to do, but since he kept walking, so did I. One foot in front of the other, like everything was normal. Like it was no freaking huge deal that Karson's arm was around my shoulders.

Why wasn't he letting go? What did this mean? Karson didn't hug me, like . . . ever. He'd elbow me or poke me or flick the end of my hair. But a hug? Did this even count?

Was this just a guy slinging his arm around the shoulder of his friend? When he'd hug Londyn, he'd wrap both arms around her. Normally his hands would dive into the back pockets of her jeans.

That was a hug. A lover's hug. This was . . . what the hell was this?

I held my shoulders as still as possible. I barely let my hands swing at my sides. If this was the only hug I got from Karson Avery, then I was making it last as long as I could.

The sun beat down on us, the afternoon rays growing stronger with every passing minute. I struggled to take a deep breath, my heart racing like a Ferrari in my chest.

Karson was relaxed. Content to leave his arm around me. His side was pressed to mine, his hand draped over my shoulder, his wrist relaxed.

He looked casual. This was a casual hug, right?

But what if I was wrong? What if this was Karson's way of testing the waters? What if he liked me? *Liked me*, liked me. What if this hug was his way of breaking past the friend zone?

Before I could make sense of my thoughts, his arm was gone and we were in town, cars whizzing by us on the street.

"What time does Aria get off work?" he asked at the stoplight.

I glanced down the road in the direction she'd walk to her restaurant. "Five."

"I'm done at six. Before the end of her shift, why don't you go to the restaurant and get her? Then come back to the car wash so we can all walk home together."

"Sure." I glanced up at his handsome profile, hoping for a sign that his hug had been . . . more.

Karson must have felt my stare. He looked down to me and those hazel eyes held me captive. My romance novels were always describing the hero holding the heroine captive with his gaze.

Totally got that one now.

Because I was pinned to the sidewalk. The air had vanished from my lungs. I was at Karson's mercy, waiting with every beat of my heart for his next move.

The breeze caught a lock of hair and blew it into my face.

Karson pulled it free from my cheek, tucking it behind my ear. His fingers skimmed the shell, sending a tickle over my skin. He swallowed hard, his Adam's apple bobbing. "I, um . . ."

Love you? Please, please let the rest of that sentence be that he loved me.

The beep of the crosswalk sounded beside us. Karson looked away, facing the street, and dropped his hand. Then he took a step forward and the moment was gone.

Stupid freaking crosswalk.

I kicked at an invisible clump of dirt, then trudged after him, hating every step that took us closer and closer to the car wash. When the sign came into view, I covered up a groan with a fake cough.

"Thrift store?" he asked.

"Yeah." I shrugged. "I guess. There's a dime in my pocket and I've got a date with Fabio."

"Need some money for a coffee or something?"

"No, thanks." While he'd swipe things here and there, he knew I wouldn't steal. He'd spent too much money on me already.

Besides, on Friday afternoons, the closest café was always packed with high school girls. They'd taken over since summer break. It was impossible to sit in there and not get overwhelmed with conversations of college and cars and clothes.

I didn't hate my life. It wasn't ideal, but I didn't hate our situation. Aria and I had our freedom and that was priceless. Living at the junkyard was better than where we'd been.

Still, listening to normal girls was painfully hard. Because if our parents hadn't died, that would have been Aria and me. We would have been the girls at a coffee shop who'd never wondered where their next meal would come from. Who didn't fear police cars that might drag them back to hell.

"I'm going to go get my new book and then find a park or something," I told Karson.

"Stay in public where people can hear you, okay?"

"I will." Other than the junkyard, I didn't go to places where someone couldn't hear me scream.

"Have fun working."

"Oh, yeah. Washing cars is my dream," he deadpanned.

I giggled and it made him smile.

He smiled so wide and bright, I refused to blink. I had to memorize that smile in the next forty-six days so that when we left California, I could take it with me.

Standing on the sidewalk, I waved and watched as he walked away. About ten feet away, he spun and grinned, giving me a mock salute. I laughed, watching his long strides and the way he walked with such grace.

Then he was gone and I left for the thrift store, taking my time over the ten-block route. There were no new additions to their very limited book supply, so next was an extra thirteen blocks to the closest library.

Not that I checked out books. I'd need a library card for that and requesting a fake one had seemed like an unnecessary risk. But I came to the library often, never speaking to the librarians, simply walking through the stacks.

There was adventure here. There was hope. There were imaginary worlds behind each dust jacket and hard spine, ready to swallow the reader whole. The smell of paper and books infused the air. The quiet whispers of patrons reminded me of fall leaves rustling on the grass.

Finally, after I'd killed another hour, I began the slow journey to Aria's restaurant. She wouldn't be ready to leave yet, but I didn't want to risk not catching her. And I hoped I could beg a lemonade with extra ice from the waitress.

She gave me two while I waited for my sister.

Aria laughed after I explained to her what was happening. "Don't you think Karson's gotten more protective lately? Do you think all big brothers are like that?"

Eww. Karson was *not* my big brother. "I don't know. Maybe."

Overprotective or not, I liked that Karson cared about our well-being. It was the one gesture that set him apart from most of the people in our lives.

"We still have an hour before he's ready," Aria said, checking the clock in the restaurant as she slung her backpack on. "Want to go somewhere?"

"Not really. I've been walking all afternoon. What if we just went and hung out at the car wash?"

"Fine by me." She said her goodbyes to her coworkers, then we made the trek to Karson's work.

There was a concrete ledge behind the row of vacuums, and Aria and I made ourselves comfortable under the shade of a tree.

I had the perfect view of Karson standing inside the metal shed with a pressure spray wand in his grip. Some days, he washed the cars. Others, he was outside, polishing the wax or running a vacuum.

It was difficult to stop myself from staring. His jeans were wet, like usual. So was his gray T-shirt. It stuck to his flat stomach. Every time he moved, the fabric seemed to stretch tighter over his shoulders and arms.

Stop staring. I had to force my eyes away, locking them on Aria, even though in my head all I could picture was Karson shirtless, wearing that towel.

Aria was telling me about her day while I fantasized about Karson. I hadn't heard a word she'd said because I was an awful sister. But then a familiar voice barked and jerked me out of my stupor.

"Stay away from me." Karson's voice filled the air.

"What the hell?" Aria muttered, twisting. Then we were both on our feet.

"That's her." I reached for my sister's arm. "Aria, that's her, isn't it?"

She took my hand, her eyes narrowing. "I don't know. Is it?"

"Yes." It was her.

The jogger from yesterday was inside the car wash, clearly ignoring the *Employees Only* sign. She was talking to Karson, waving her hands wildly as he lifted an arm and pointed toward the exit.

"Go. Away." Another shout that carried our way.

The woman didn't budge. She crossed her arms over her chest, planting her legs wide.

Karson clenched his jaw, then stormed into the office and slammed the door behind him.

The woman didn't notice us watching. She scowled and marched to her car. With a snap of her fingers, she ordered away the guy drying it with a towel. Then she was behind the wheel and on the road, her tires squealing as she raced onto the street.

I didn't wait for my sister as I rushed to the office, almost at the door when it flew open and Karson stalked outside.

He spotted me and changed direction. "Hey."

"Karson, that was her. The jogger."

"What?"

"Yes, that was her. I'm sure."

"Fuck."

"Who is that woman?" I asked as Aria joined us.

Karson gritted his teeth and stared at the road where she'd disappeared. "My mother."

CHAPTER FIVE

CLARA

"Hey." I smiled at Karson as he came striding my way. I was outside the van, shaking the remainder of the cat food from the bag into a bowl for the stray.

The bag that I'd bought over a month and a half ago, the day we'd seen Karson's mother jogging down our road, had lasted a long time. Too long. Katherine's cat hadn't been coming around much, probably because Katherine wasn't here.

"Hey," he said. "Where's Aria?"

"Shower." I crumpled the bag into a ball for Lou's metal trash can. "She's been working on her plants all day, getting them ready for when we go. She wants to stage them around Lou's place as a goodbye present."

Karson nodded and sank onto an old car hood. It rested on top of a heap of large metal scraps and a rusted wheel well. The hood was our equivalent of a living room chair.

"How was work?" I asked. While Aria and I hadn't had to work today, he'd gone in for an eight-hour shift at the car wash.

"Work." He shrugged, but the lines on his forehead spoke volumes about his day.

And who'd paid him a visit.

"She was there again, wasn't she?"

"Yeah," he muttered. "Came right before I clocked out."

In the time since Karson's mother had made her first appearance at the car wash, she'd continued to confront him at least once a week.

"What did she want?"

He lifted a shoulder. "Didn't let her catch me. The second I saw her car, I shut myself in the office."

"Does your boss care?"

"I mean, he doesn't like it. But he gets it."

I gave him a sad smile. "Sorry."

"Yeah. Whatever. She can fuck off."

Karson hadn't spoken about his mother. Not since her first visit and not before. In all the years that we'd lived together, he hadn't elaborated. Just like me. What I knew of his past were bits and pieces. Karson's mother had been an alcoholic. Maybe she still was. And she'd been a bitch, according to her son. That obviously hadn't changed. But I didn't know exactly what had happened to make him run away.

The best decision of my life. A phrase he'd repeated countless times.

"Anyway"—he stood—"wanted to let you know I was back."

"Oh, okay."

He walked away, his shoulders tight and his hands shoved into his jeans pockets.

Karson had withdrawn from me over the past month and a half. Every visit from his mother sent him deeper and deeper into himself. He rarely ate with us these days. He walked us to and from town, but the trips were quiet and tense.

Gone was the playful Karson who'd tease and flirt. Gone was the Karson who'd put his arm around my shoulders. Gone was the Karson who'd looked at me at the stoplight like maybe he wanted to kiss me.

I was losing him.

And there were only three days left.

The hope I had of seeing him again after we left this place was dwindling like the numbers on the truck's wall.

I struggled to find any excitement at all for Las Vegas. For the first time, I didn't want to go. I didn't want to leave here and leave him.

Regardless, I'd packed. Aria and I were both preparing to leave. Ready or not, time was running out, and I had to move on with my life. Most of what we'd done today had been to organize our belongings.

We'd be taking a bus to Vegas. Four days ago, we'd gone to the station to ask about tickets and get the schedule. There would be room enough for us to each take two backpacks. Today, I'd packed the keepers and set out the clothes I was leaving behind. I'd be wearing them for the next three days, like my shirt today. It was a favorite but the hem was frayed and there was a hole in the armpit. Aria and I had decided that wrinkled jeans and tattered shirts were worth wearing now, so that when the time came, we were loaded to leave with our best stuff.

"Come smell me." Aria emerged from the maze, her hair wet and a towel looped over her arm.

"Why am I smelling you?"

"Because I smell awesome." She smiled and came close, putting an arm around my shoulders.

I scrunched up my nose. "You did use soap, didn't you?"

"Huh?" She stepped back and sniffed her underarm.

I giggled. "Kidding. You smell great."

"It's that new shampoo I got at the dollar store. I love that it smells like a flower. From now on, that's going to be my smell."

"Flowers?"

She nodded. "Yup."

"Good choice." My favorite smell was orange and vanilla. It reminded me of Creamsicles, the ones Dad used to buy us on hot summer days from an ice cream truck. But I still hadn't found a soap that smelled just right. Probably because there were only so many options at the dollar store. Maybe when I had a job and some money, I could go to a beauty store and buy my smell.

"What do you want to do for dinner?" Aria asked, hanging up her towel on our "hook." It was just a hinge in the truck door, but it worked.

"Should we have peanut butter and honey sandwiches? Or honey and peanut butter sandwiches?"

"Hmm." She tapped her chin. "Peanut butter and honey is fancier than honey and peanut butter, and I'm feeling fancy tonight."

"Then allow me to cook for you, madam."

"And fetch me our best champagne."

"But of course." I feigned a bow and hopped into the truck, going to the food stash. With our one and only butter knife, I made us each a sandwich.

"Is Karson back?" Aria asked, taking a bite after handing me a bottle of lukewarm water.

"Yeah. He came over when you were in the shower. She was there again today."

"Bitch," she muttered.

"Has he said anything to you?"

Aria shook her head. "No. But he doesn't talk to me like he talks to you."

"I might make him a sandwich. See if he's okay."

"Fine by me. This bread is about done anyway." There was no mold, but the crust was hard and dry.

We ate in comfortable silence and when I was done, I made Karson's sandwich. When I left, Aria was settled on her bed with a book on her lap, braiding her hair into a long rope.

A nervous flutter settled in my belly as I walked toward Karson's tent. The flap on the door was open but I knocked on the wall anyway. "Hey. It's me."

"Hey." Karson sat in the main room with a deck of cards spread out in a game of solitaire.

The sight of him playing alone broke my heart.

Karson had been alone a lot this past year. When Londyn had lived here, she'd been his constant companion. Best friends. And though Aria and I were here, it wasn't the same.

I'd always be grateful to my parents that I'd been born with my best friend. Even on the darkest days, I was never alone. I always had Aria.

"Want to play a game?" I settled across from him on the floor.

"Sure."

"Here." I handed him the sandwich. "Dinner."

"Thanks." He took it and chomped a huge bite. "Mmm. Peanut butter and honey. I haven't had this in *so* long."

I laughed. "Like a day?"

"Two." He chewed, a grin forming on his lips.

"What are we playing?" I asked, scooping up the cards.

"You beat me at both gin and poker last time, so a rematch of either would be good."

"Gin." I dealt the cards.

He swiped his hands clean after demolishing the sandwich, then picked up his hand. "One of the guys at work bought me beer."

I blinked, stunned by the admission. "Really?"

"It's not the first time."

"Oh." How had I missed that? "Do you, um . . . drink a lot?"

"Nah. I am not about becoming my mother."

Right. He'd mentioned once that she'd get really nasty after too many vodkas.

"I brought the six-pack home with me. Want one?"

"Um . . ." Why did this feel like breaking the rules? *Because it was.* Despite my current living situation and the fact that we were basically trespassing, I still tried to follow the rules. Even in the beginning when we hadn't been able to get good jobs, Aria and I had never stolen food like he did. "I've never had a drink before."

"You don't have to." Karson stretched behind him, reaching past the partition to his room. Then he lifted the six-pack and set it down at his side.

The cans were white with red letters. The tops were a shade of brassy gold. Karson plucked one from the plastic rings and the top hissed as he popped it.

"I guess . . . I'll try it." My voice cracked a little with the thrill.

He handed over the can, then opened his own to raise in the air. "Cheers."

"Cheers." I tipped the can to my lips and sipped. And gagged. "Gross."

He chuckled, swallowing his own gulp. "It's different."

"If different and horrible mean the same thing, then yes, it's different."

The smile that stretched across Karson's face was worth the nasty beer. His laugh boomed through the tent, drowning the fears I'd had of losing him.

"You haven't smiled much lately," I said.

He sighed and took another drink. "No, I haven't."

"Are you okay? This thing with your mom . . ."

"I don't understand why she can't let me go. She didn't want me years ago when I actually needed her. Now she comes looking for me? Now? What the fuck? Why?"

"Maybe you need to hear her out."

He scowled as he took another drink.

Okay. Bad suggestion. I sipped from my own can, the second taste not as bitter and startling as the first. "Sorry."

"It's not your fault. I'm being a dick. Sorry. I just don't want anything to do with her."

"You never talk about your home with her."

"You never talk about yours either." Karson's hazel gaze locked on mine. In it, the silent plea to trust him broke any resolve I'd had to keep my past hidden.

So I took another drink, and told him the story that only Aria knew.

"Our uncle is a sick son of a bitch. After our parents died, we went into foster care for a while, waiting until they could figure out what to do with us. My parents didn't have a plan for us."

Parents did that for their kids, right? Planned for the worst? I'd heard our social worker say a few times that our parents hadn't had a will. They should have.

"We ended up with our uncle. He was Mom's stepbrother. I didn't even know we had an uncle until after Mom and Dad . . ." I didn't like to say it. Seven years later and I didn't like to say that they'd died.

"Maybe we shouldn't talk about this. I don't want it to hurt you, Clara."

I met his worried gaze. "If there's anyone I'd want to tell for the first time, it's you."

"Okay." He nodded toward my beer.

I took another drink, letting the carbonation tickle my tongue. "My grandma had Mom before she married Craig's dad. I guess that made him my grandpa too, not that I knew him. He died before I met him. My grandma too, when I was a baby. I only remember her face from pictures."

And even then, the pictures were fading. Some nights I'd wake up in a cold sweat because I couldn't remember what Mom and Dad had looked like either. What their laughs had sounded like. Aria and I had a few pictures, but even with them, the memories were fuzzy.

"My dad's parents, my other grandparents, live outside of Phoenix. They have a pool we played in whenever we visited. Before."

"Why didn't you go live with them?" Karson asked.

"They didn't want us. Craig did. I don't think my grandparents knew about him. What he was."

Craig had been a different guy then. Kind. Gentle. Fake. I remembered him meeting us, crouching down and shaking our hands. I remembered him saying how pretty we were and how much we reminded him of Mom. He'd given us stuffed teddy bears that day and a pack of M&M's to split.

"He'd put on a good show for the social workers. They believed it. He was younger than my grandparents, and since he lived here in Temecula, I guess all the adults thought it made sense not to move us."

"Stupid fuckers."

"Yeah." I huffed, taking another drink. Warmth spread through my chest, making it easier to talk. Maybe it was the beer. Or maybe it was just Karson. "He just wanted their money. Mom and Dad's. He took everything. The house. The furniture. Our toys. If he could sell it, he did. Then he moved us into that shitty trailer and kept the money for himself. By the time we ran away, it was pretty much gone."

"What did he do with it? Drugs?"

I lifted a shoulder. "Maybe. I know he gambled because one night this guy showed up and broke down the front door. He had a gun and told Craig that if he didn't pay his gambling debt, he was dead."

Part of me still wished it had ended that night. That Craig had had a roll of cash in his pocket and that guy had fired the gun.

"He used to throw parties while Aria and I hid out in our room. We couldn't even lock the door because it was broken. And I think . . ." I took in a deep breath, bracing myself for the realization it had taken me a while to understand. "I think there was a reason Mom didn't let us see Craig. That she didn't talk about him."

Karson's spine stiffened. "What?"

"He was a jerk and didn't give a shit about us most of the time. But since there was food and Aria and I could take care of ourselves, it didn't matter. Then it got creepy. We turned fourteen and got, um . . . boobs." I grimaced, not wanting to say that word to Karson. "He stared at us. A lot. He'd touch us too much."

A chill crept over my skin. A sour taste spread across my mouth, so I chased it down with another gulp of beer.

"Eventually it was so disgusting that we started packing. We knew Londyn had run away. Why not us too?"

"She was here then, right?"

I nodded. "Yeah. We were trying to save up as much as we could first, not sure what kind of jobs we'd be able to get since we were only fifteen. But then he came after Aria."

The tent went eerily still. Karson sat like a rock but the fury pulsing off his body was like a heat wave.

"He didn't, like . . ." *Rape.* I couldn't say that word either. "He touched her. He ripped her shirt. He got her pants open. I didn't even know it was happening. I was in the bathroom but then I heard her scream and by the time I came running out, she'd already fought her way free."

I closed my eyes and heard the echo of her scream. It haunted me. I expected it always would.

"I'll fucking kill him." Karson moved so fast, I blinked and he was out the tent's door.

"No!" I scrambled to my feet, running to catch up. "Karson, stop."

"He's dead."

"Karson." I caught up to him by the small gate, grabbing his elbow with both of my hands. "Don't. If you go there, what are you going to do?"

"Kill him."

"And then who will be here with us?" I asked gently. Karson would go kill Craig. He had that sort of rage inside of him.

His body tensed but he stopped fighting my grip.

"It was a long time ago," I said.

"Doesn't make it fucking right."

I sighed. "I know. But if you go there and do something reckless, he wins. Please, please don't."

He seethed for a full minute before he backed away from the fence. Then he faced me, planting his hands on his hips. "Did he touch you too?"

"No. We ran and shut ourselves in the bedroom. He pounded on the door for hours, but we held him off." Aria and I had braced our backs against the door and our feet against a bed, then pushed with all our might. By the time the pounding and Craig's bellowing had stopped, my legs had lost all their strength. Well, nearly all.

Never in my life had I wished so hard for my parents. I'd silently begged Mom and Dad to appear, for us to wake up from the nightmare and be home in our beds with them sleeping down the hallway.

I wished for them a lot, during the hard days. Aria seemed so angry at them sometimes. She never said it, but I could tell she was mad at them for leaving us—for leaving us vulnerable to a man like Craig.

She had a right to be angry, and there were times when I felt that too. But mostly . . . I just missed Mom's smile and gentle voice. I missed Dad's loud laugh and how he'd scoop us into his arms every evening when he'd come home from work.

I wished for them even though I knew that wish wouldn't come true.

"Then what?" Karson asked.

"Craig gave up eventually. And when he did, we climbed out the window before dawn with our backpacks and supplies, then came here."

"Clara." The pain on his handsome face broke my heart.

"I'm okay, Karson."

Without warning, he pulled me into his chest, wrapping his arms around me tight. "I fucking hate him."

"Me too." I dragged in a long breath of his shirt. He smelled of soap and earth and Karson. My Karson. My arms snaked around his waist, and I hugged him. A real hug, with his cheek resting on my hair.

Until he loosened his hold and tipped my chin up to his face. "I'm sorry."

"Don't be."

"I shouldn't have brought it up. We should have just played cards and had fun."

"We can still do that. If you want." I hooked a thumb toward the tent. "Your beer is growing on me."

"Only you could make me smile right now." He chuckled and put an arm around my shoulders, then he steered me for the tent.

We played gin and pretended we weren't living in a junkyard. We drank beers like other teenaged kids did to break the rules and push the boundaries.

"My lips are numb." I dabbed my lower lip, flicking it with my index finger.

Karson laughed. "I don't feel anything yet."

"Really?" Was I slurring? "I feel . . . good. Aria is going to be mad that we left her out."

"She can have the rest of mine." He shrugged and

surged to his feet. But he'd forgotten that he couldn't stand in the center of the tent and he wacked his head on the roof. "Ow."

I burst out laughing. "I thought you weren't feeling anything."

"I guess I am now." He swayed on his feet. While I'd only had a beer and a half, Karson had nearly gone through the other four.

"She's probably asleep." I got to my feet, extending my arms like an airplane to find my balance. When one of my hands landed on Karson's hot skin, I clung to his forearm, not shy about touching him. Not tonight.

What did they call alcohol? Liquid courage? I got that reference now.

My smile pinched my cheeks as I tugged Karson out of the tent. The air outside was still warm, even as the sun dipped below the horizon. The stars were just beginning to show in the royal blue sky.

"Want to watch for shooting stars?" I asked, walking toward the Cadillac. "We can make a game out of it. First one to three wins."

"What about Aria?"

No light was coming from inside the truck. She'd always been an early riser and tended to go to bed before dark. That or she was hunkered under a blanket, consuming her book by flashlight. "She's probably asleep."

"'Kay. Stargazing it is." Karson climbed onto the Cadillac's wide hood, leaning so his back was against the windshield. Then he raised his arms and placed them beneath his head.

I scrambled to his side, settling against the metal. My jeans and shirt were going to be filthy, but in my happily beer-buzzed state, I didn't care. These were short-term clothes anyway.

"I can't believe you suck so much at gin *and* poker." I barely got the sentence out before I broke into a fit of giggles.

"You should be saying thank you."

"For what?"

"For letting you win."

I scoffed. "You did not let me win."

He stayed quiet, his gaze on the sky.

"Did you let me win?"

Still, no response.

I shifted, pushing up on an arm to look down at him. "Karson."

"Clara."

"Did you let me win?"

He looked over and winked. "You'll never know."

"Jerk!" I poked him in the side, then lay down again, my smile wider now than it had been all night.

He chuckled. If that was what I could do for him, make him laugh, then I was calling tonight a success. And maybe I needed a laugh too.

I was lighter, having told him my story. The fear that came with it had eased. Maybe I should have told him a long time ago.

"I know it's not ideal, but I'm going to miss these starry nights," Karson said.

"Me too."

The junkyard was far enough from the center of town that the glow from the city's lights didn't completely obscure the night sky. The stars would come out and on clear nights like this, they were little blips of hope, twinkles of joy that promised life wouldn't always be this hard. They were there, watching over us. Maybe the stars were the lost souls of the ones we'd loved.

Maybe two of those stars were for my parents.

I hoped at this very moment, with me lying beside the boy I really liked, Dad wasn't watching.

"I'm not going to miss the dirt," he said.

"Same. And I'm not going to miss the tight spaces. Sleeping in an oversized coffin. Someday, I want a house with lots of windows. So that even when I'm inside, it feels open and airy."

"I just want four walls. Four real walls. A fridge. A microwave."

I snuck a glance at Karson's profile. It was perfection. His nose was straight. His jaw strong and dusted with stubble. His lips soft.

"I'm going to miss you." The words came out before I could stop them.

When he faced me, his hazel eyes had that captivating edge again. The same one he'd given me the day of the stoplight. "I'm going to miss you too."

My breath caught in my throat.

"Clara..."

"Yeah?"

Karson didn't answer. He turned to the sky and my heart sank. I was imagining this. It had to be the beer. It had to be—

I didn't get to finish that thought. Because one moment, my eyes were glued to the darkening night sky.

The next, Karson was there.

And his lips came crashing down on mine.

CHAPTER SIX
CLARA

The rattle of metal on metal woke me from sleep.

I blinked, wincing at the ache pounding in my temples. God, it was hot. Why was it so hot?

A weight rested on my side, and behind me, there was a furnace. A hard, strong furnace.

No, a body.

I gasped and sat up, scrambling out of Karson's hold. *Tent.* We were in the tent. We were in his . . . bed.

He stirred, cracking open his eyes. Then he stretched an arm over his head and the movement caused his shirt to ride up, revealing a peek at those washboard abs. "Morning."

"Morning." I gulped and looked down at myself. Still clothed. Then last night came rushing back.

The Cadillac. The stars. The beers.

The kiss.

We'd come back to the tent after Karson had kissed me.

Oh my God. Karson had kissed me. A lot. He'd kissed me a lot, *a lot*.

My fingertips drifted to my swollen lips. *Holy. Shit.*

Karson Avery had kissed me. I held back a squeal.

The shock on my face must have woken Karson up completely because he sat up, his eyes on alert. "Clara."

"You kissed me."

He nodded. "That's all that happened."

That's all? It was a kiss. A freaking kiss. Something I'd wanted for months and months and months. "I remember."

"Are you—"

"Good. Great! I'm great. Except I have a headache." Though I couldn't tell if the spinning was because I was experiencing my first hangover or because of the kiss.

"Yeah." He ran a hand through his hair. "I do too."

What did we do now? There was no way I'd be kissing him again until I brushed my teeth. My mouth was dry and tasted . . . blech. Beer breath was awful. Though I didn't have a mirror, my hair was most certainly a mess.

Aria was going to take one look at me and . . . know. *Oh my God.* My stomach pitched. She was going to know. There was no way I'd be able to hide my puffy lips and this perma-grin from my sister. My secret crush was about to be the talk of the junkyard.

My head throbbed as I forced myself to unsteady feet. "I'd better go."

"Clara, wait."

I didn't stop moving. "Thanks for the, um . . . see ya."

Leaving him in the tent, I hurried outside and into the bright morning sun. I winced as my temples pounded but dragged in some air and put one foot in front of the other. When I passed the Cadillac, I kept my gaze on the path, refusing to let myself look at the hood.

The hood where Karson had kissed me.

What did this mean? This was a good thing, right? Karson. Avery. Kissed. Me.

Except at the moment, I kind of wanted to hurl. Pressing a hand to my stomach, I hustled to the truck, hopped in and gathered my towel and shower supplies.

"Morning." Aria was on her bed with the novel she'd had last night.

"Hi. Sorry. I was in the tent. I, uh, fell asleep."

She shrugged. "I figured. I crashed early. This book wasn't good enough to stay up late with."

I ducked my chin, hoping to keep my face hidden until I could assess the damage. Luckily, my hair was hanging everywhere like a curtain. "I'm taking a shower."

"'Kay."

Before she could say anything else, I disappeared, rushing for the shop. The smell of grease and gasoline made me gag, but I locked myself in the bathroom and cranked the shower on hot. Then as steam flooded the room, I faced the mirror.

Yep. Swollen lips.

A laugh escaped as I leaned closer, taking them in. Karson had kissed me. I had kissed him. We'd had a full-on make-out session on the Cadillac. Londyn's Cadillac.

Would she hate me for it? Would she hate me for loving Karson? A wave of guilt swept over my shoulders, but I shook it away.

"She'll never know," I whispered, then went for my toothbrush, scrubbing my mouth until all I tasted was mint.

The mirror began to fog so I stripped off yesterday's clothes and stepped into the shower stall. I lingered, soaking in the warmth and letting it chase away the hangover. At least . . . I assumed it was a hangover. By the time I stepped out, my headache wasn't as bad and my mind was clear.

I'd need a clear head. Because I'd bolted on Karson and we had to talk about the kissing.

Would he want to do it again? Or would he say it was a mistake? I was fairly certain I'd die if he told me I was a mistake.

We only had two days left until our birthday. They'd be the longest two days of my life if Karson rejected me now.

Aria was dressed and eating a rice cake when I

returned to the truck. She was sitting on the end, kicking her legs.

"I tried beer," I blurted, climbing inside. I put my soap and shampoo away, then hung up my towel. Then I sat beside her and let my head rest on her shoulder. "Beer is really bad."

She laughed. "Where'd you get beer?"

"Karson. Some guy at his work bought him a six-pack."

"Ahh." She nodded. "Was that why you fell asleep in the tent?"

"Yeah." I sighed, holding back the rest of the story. I wasn't ready to admit my feelings. I wasn't ready to admit that I'd betrayed Londyn by falling in love with her boyfriend—ex-boyfriend.

"I thought maybe you and Karson . . ."

"Huh?" My heart dropped as I feigned confusion.

"Do you like him?"

"We're friends." I sat up straight. Not a complete lie. Then I stood and walked to the truck's wall, picking up the dry-erase marker to write today's number.

Two.

Only two days left and I'd say goodbye to Karson. Kiss or not, we were going our separate ways. Maybe his kiss had been a farewell.

"What time do you want to head in for work?" I asked after swallowing the lump in my throat.

"About an hour. But you don't have to come with me. I

doubt Karson's mother wants anything to do with us. I think she was just looking for him."

"Yeah." We'd explained that much to Karson, but he still insisted on escorting us into town.

"I'm actually going to head out when he's not looking." She smirked. "See you later."

"Be careful." Before she could jump down, I went and wrapped my arms around her. "Love you."

"Love you too. Enjoy your day off. Will you—"

"Water your plants? Of course."

She snatched her empty backpack, then jumped down and scanned the plant buckets that surrounded the truck. The happy smile on her face disappeared as she took in the flowers and green leaves.

Those were her babies and there was no way for them to come to Vegas. They'd probably die before fall—never something I'd say aloud. But Lou wasn't going to care for them.

The man only had so much to give, though what he'd given us had been enough.

"Bye." She waved, then headed out, hooking the pack's straps on her shoulders as she walked.

"Turkey if you bring home a sandwich," I called to her back.

She lifted a hand with a thumb up.

Two days, then there'd be no more scrap sandwiches. Well, after we got on our feet.

Aria and I weren't delusional about what waited for us

at the end of our countdown. The days were likely to get harder for a while as we started a new life. Without jobs or a home, I imagined we'd be spending a week or two in a sleezy motel with bedbugs and cockroaches.

But that was what we'd been saving for. We had enough money to afford a cheap room while we got an apartment lined up. Neither of us wanted to be living on the streets, especially in Las Vegas.

The sudden urge to count our savings stash came over me, and I hurried to my bed, taking it out and separating the cash into piles.

Two thousand three hundred and fifty dollars. Exactly what had been there the last time Aria and I had counted it out. Nearly three years of peanut butter and honey sandwiches, eating whatever our respective restaurants would give us and spending next to nothing, all so we could have a decent shot at a future.

Please, let it be enough.

I returned the money to the bag and stowed it in its hiding place. My stomach growled, driving me to the foodstuffs. Bent over the supplies, I was debating my limited options when Karson knocked on the truck. "Hey."

"Hi." I blushed.

He held up two rolled tortillas, probably with peanut butter and banana inside. That was a staple breakfast around here. "Since you brought me dinner."

"Thanks."

He hopped into the truck, handing one of the rollups over, then we sat down and ate.

Meals here were without fanfare and took only moments. I wished there was more to do because by the time I'd chewed the last bite, I still didn't know what to say.

"Where's Aria?" he asked.

"Work. She left." Probably while he'd been in the shower. The strands of his dark hair were damp and finger combed.

"She should have waited."

"She'll be fine." I waved it off. "Why would your mom want anything to do with us?"

"Who knows?" He frowned. "But she's fucking crazy, so . . ."

I waited for more, but he let that sentence hang, and with it my hopes that he'd tell me about his past. I'd confided in him. Would he ever trust me with his story?

"I need to head in and grab my paycheck. Cash it at the bank. Want to come?" he asked.

"Sure. But I'd better water Aria's plants first."

"'Kay." He stood up. "I'll help."

Thirty minutes later, after working and most definitely *not* talking about the kiss, Karson and I were on the road to town.

"Want a coffee or something?" he asked. "My treat. I'm definitely getting one because my head goddamn hurts. Fucking beer."

I giggled. "Should have stuck to two, like me."

"How are you feeling?"

Confused. Happy. Anxious. Sad. Take your pick. "Fine. Better after my shower."

"That's good."

And that was the end of our conversation about last night, apparently. The only sound between us was the smack of our shoes on the street and sidewalk. When we got to the nearest café, Karson led the way inside, going to the counter, where a display case flaunted baked goods.

"Two black coffees," he ordered. "To go."

The waitress nodded, quickly filled a pair of white paper cups and pressed on black plastic lids. Then we got out of there before the smell of sugar and butter and muffins and cookies became too tempting.

He groaned as we walked out the door. "God, those cookies smelled good. I almost swiped two. Proud of me for not stealing?"

"Very." I nodded. "I want to learn how to bake one day. When I have a kitchen. I remember my mom baked a lot. Aria and I would help her in the kitchen by dumping ingredients into the bowl after she'd measure them out."

"What's your favorite type of cookie?" Karson sipped his coffee.

"Ginger molasses. Or pumpkin chocolate chip."

"I don't think I've ever had those."

"Seriously?"

He shrugged. "My mom wasn't much for baking. Or

cooking. Or doing anything but drowning in a bottle of vodka."

"Sorry."

He waved it off and took another sip.

I took a drink, cringing at the bitter flavor. Coffee had never appealed. Maybe it would as I got older, but I'd still drink it because Karson had spent a dollar. And because it gave me something to do.

I was coming out of my skin here. How could he be so calm? So normal? Was this how he wanted to act? Like nothing had happened? Maybe pretend it was just nothing?

My insides clenched. He regretted it. That had to be the answer. He regretted the kiss. I was a mistake.

Ugh. I was blaming beer for this.

I bit my lip as we walked, determined not to cry. We made our way toward the car wash but when we passed a small park, Karson nodded for me to follow him across the grass toward a bench. "Let's sit. Drink our coffee."

The park was empty, probably because it was still early. In the afternoons, there were always mothers pushing kids on the swing set and watching as they zoomed down the slide.

Karson and I sat on the bench, a visible space between us. "Guess we should probably talk about last night."

"Yeah?" I held my breath.

"I'm not going to apologize for kissing you."

The air rushed from my lungs. "I wasn't sure if you might, um . . . regret it, maybe?"

"What? Never. Do you?"

My heart skipped and I shook my head. "Never."

"Good." His shoulders relaxed and he lifted his cup to his lips.

"But . . ." The cup froze in midair. "Is this, like, a rebound thing?"

It had taken every ounce of courage I had to ask that question.

Karson shifted to face me as he set his coffee on the ground. Then he moved, closing the gap between us, until his thigh brushed mine. His arm went to the back of the bench. "No. Definitely not a rebound."

"Are you sure? You and Londyn were together for a long time."

"I'm sure. Londyn and I were better friends than we were a couple. It was over the day she left." Karson raised his hand and his fingers sifted into my hair, brushing it away from my ear.

My breath hitched.

Then his mouth was there, hovering over mine. Karson brushed his lips across mine, teasing, and then he pressed in deep, his arms wrapping around my shoulders.

My cup of coffee fell out of my hand, landing on the grass beside our feet. I didn't care. I didn't think. Like last night, I just let Karson kiss me.

His tongue ran across my lower lip, and I opened so he

could sweep inside. Karson pressed closer, the heat from his body soaking into mine. Our tongues tangled and twisted. Every breathless second was bliss and when he finally broke away, I was lost in the darkened green and gold swirls of his eyes.

Karson wanted me. Me.

"Why?" I hadn't meant to voice my insecurity, but that damn word had slipped out.

"Why what?"

I closed my eyes and braced. "Are you kissing me because we only have two days left?"

"Clara, look at me." His fingers tugged on a strand of hair that hung between us. He twirled it around his index finger as I lifted my lashes. "I'm kissing you, wishing I had kissed you *two hundred* and two days ago."

I practically slid off the bench as I melted. If not for his arms still around me, I would have joined my coffee as a puddle in the grass. "Really?"

He leaned in and brushed his lips across mine, whispering, "Really."

The next kiss was a lot like I'd remembered from last night. Fumbling hands. Wet lips. Tentative nips and licks as I learned more about what he liked. What I liked. His coffee was forgotten as we clung to each other, sitting on the park bench, kissing like we were the only people in the world. It was only when the shout of a child rang through the air that we broke apart.

My lips were raw and puffy again. Karson inched

away, drawing in a few pained breaths. I ducked my chin to hide a smile because there was a noticeable bulge beneath his jeans.

"Need to go anywhere else?" Karson asked, finally standing from the bench.

"No." I took his outstretched hand and stood, letting him lace our fingers together. Then we walked, our arms swinging between us, to the car wash. "Do you think all beer tastes like that stuff last night?"

Karson laughed. "Probably."

"Yuck." I faked a gag as we rounded the block. "I'll stick with lemonade, thanks."

"Same here. With ice. Lots and lots of ice."

"And ice cream."

"With chocolate syr—" Karson froze, his tennis shoes slapping to a stop.

"What?" I followed his gaze to the car wash's parking lot.

And there she was. His mother.

She was in jeans and a gray button-down shirt. Her hands waved in the air as she spoke to Karson's boss, who stood with his arms crossed over his chest and his mouth glued shut.

But it wasn't Karson's mother or his boss that sent a jolt of panic through my veins.

It was the uniformed police officer standing between them who sent my heart into my throat.

The officer looked up and spotted us. He narrowed his

gaze and cocked his head. The movement caused Karson's mother to stop speaking. She turned and her eyes widened. Then her hand was in the air, shaking a pointed finger.

Karson kept a firm hold on my hand as he took a step backward.

"Run."

CHAPTER SEVEN

CLARA

"Do you think they followed us?" I panted. There was a kink in my neck from constantly checking over my shoulder as we'd raced home.

Karson had led the way. He'd taken us in circles around the blocks surrounding the car wash. Then we'd jogged down alleyways and cut through unfenced yards. Finally, after an hour, we'd decided to head to Aria's work and wait until the end of her shift.

After she'd clocked out, we'd given her a fast explanation that Karson's mother had brought in the police.

"I don't think so." Aria's cheeks were flushed, and her forehead was covered in sweat as she cast one last look down the road toward town. Then she stepped through the gate with us and into the safety of the junkyard.

"Why would she talk to the cops?" I asked Karson.

He kicked at the dirt. "Fuck."

"Karson, why?"

He didn't answer me.

Adrenaline had been coursing through my system for hours and suddenly, it felt like my legs were too weak to hold me up. My head started swimming. My chest felt too tight.

"Clara." My sister put her hand on my shoulder. "Are you okay?"

I shook my head. "Can't breathe."

"Hey." Karson put his hand on my other shoulder. "In and out. Do it. Breathe in."

I obeyed.

"And out."

I followed his order again but still felt like crashing.

"Do it again. In and out, Clara. In and out."

I closed my eyes and listened to his voice, letting it soothe the panic. It had been a long time since I'd freaked out like this. The last time had been after our parents' accident.

When the ground beneath my feet no longer felt like it was giving way, I cracked my eyelids.

"You okay?" Aria asked.

"Yeah. Sorry."

"Don't be." She took my hand in hers, then shot a scowl at Karson. "What is going on with your mother?"

He sighed, let me go and jerked his chin to the tent.

Aria and I followed as he walked away, the three of us congregating in his place.

Karson dragged a hand through his hair. "She wants me to come home."

"But why?" I asked.

He shrugged. "Because she's fucking crazy? I don't know. The last time she came to work, she begged me to come home."

"You're nineteen." I tossed out a hand. "Isn't she, like, three years too late?"

He scoffed. "She doesn't want me to come home so she can act like a mother. She wants me to come home because I *am* nineteen and can get a decent job. She wants me to be her paycheck."

"She said that?" Aria asked.

Karson shook his head. "She didn't have to. I know her well enough to understand how she operates. It's all lies and manipulations. The second time she stopped by, she'd promised that she'd stopped drinking and wanted to make amends. The next visit, I could smell the booze on her breath when she asked me for a loan. She's never been able to hold down a job, and she's desperate. Somehow she stumbled onto where I work so she's out to make my life hell."

"But she has a nice car," I said. "Those jogging clothes were fancy."

"My guess? After I ran away, she found a guy to take care of her. Gave him some sob story or something. She was always good at that. Making men feel like they could rescue her. He probably tossed her and now she's looking for the next fucking idiot to leech from. That idiot just isn't going to be me."

That was more than he'd ever told us. Karson's words were so bitter. Pain and anger infused his tone and made me ache.

"You're sure?" Aria asked.

He shrugged. "No, but it's an educated guess. She's been doing shit like this my whole life."

"Okay, what now?" I asked. "She came jogging down our road. She has to know that you're living here."

"Maybe. But if she knew, Lou's fence and padlock wouldn't stop her. My guess is she heard a rumor I was here but doesn't know for sure. And the car wash is open to the public."

Not surrounded by chain link and razor wire.

"She saw us together today. She saw me walking. It doesn't take much to know we're together and living around here."

He dropped his gaze to the floor and nodded. "We could be at any of the houses on this road. But it doesn't matter. There's nothing she can do. Eventually, she'll realize that I'm not playing her fucked-up games and move on."

"There's nothing she can do to *you*," Aria said. "You're nineteen. But we're seventeen."

"Only for a couple days."

"Two days. Two years. It doesn't matter." She held up her chin. "If the cops find us, they'll send us back to our uncle's house and I won't go back. Not for two seconds."

I took Aria's hand and squeezed it tight. "We're not going back."

"She'll go away," Karson promised. "Two more days."

That number should have brought me comfort, but instead, my heart lurched. Two more days, forty-eight hours, and we'd go our separate ways.

"Well, I'm going to take a shower." Aria stood up. "I stink like grease."

I stayed on the floor, waiting until she left us alone, then I put my hand on Karson's forearm. "Are you okay?"

"I'm pissed." His jaw clenched. "I hate her. I fucking hate her, Clara."

"Want to talk about it?" I held my breath, hoping he'd open up.

He picked up my hand, but not to shrug off my touch. He played with my fingers, tracing them with his own. He pressed our palms together. He circled our thumbs. "She's a pathological liar. She's a drunk. She hates me."

"I'm sorry."

"But it's nothing, you know? Nothing compared to what the rest of you had to live with."

Oh my God. It suddenly made sense. "That's why you don't talk about it? Because you think it's not bad enough?"

"I brought a lot of trouble onto myself. It's not the

same. Londyn's parents were junkies. Gemma's mother did some fucked-up shit to her. Katherine's too. What your uncle did to you and Aria is sick. You guys . . . you survived so much."

"So did you."

"No." He caressed my knuckles with the pad of his thumb. "Nothing like that."

"I'd like to know what happened with your mom. If you want to talk."

His frame deflated. "She's a drunk. She hides it from boyfriends so she can use them for whatever she needs. She's got a fake face for the world but the real one comes out behind closed doors. I got the real one."

"Did she hurt you?"

"She didn't give a fuck about me. She'd cook me a meal and tell me I didn't deserve to eat it. She'd see me watching TV and tell me she hated the sight of me in her house. When I was little, I did everything to please her. I'd clean. I'd get good grades. I'd help her to bed when she was piss drunk. And the whole time, she'd tell me I was dog shit."

"Karson." Oh my God. How could he think what he'd been through wasn't horrific?

"You know what though, I am a screwup."

"What are you talking about? Of course you're not."

"No, she was right about one thing. I fuck up everything I touch."

My jaw dropped. "What are you talking about?"

"A lot of her problems are because of me."

"How?"

He rubbed at an invisible spot on his jeans, hesitating long enough that I held my breath, worried about what he'd say. "A while back, before I ran away, I got into some trouble. Me and some friends went out one night. We'd been drinking and smoking pot. We found this old warehouse, not that far from here actually. One of the guys had a can of spray paint. He drew a dick on the wall. Me and the others found some rocks and threw them through the windows."

I bit my tongue. I wanted so badly not to picture him there. To see him doing those things. But Karson had always had a reckless edge. There was anger in him and defiance. Most of the time he kept it hidden, especially when we were here and it was just us. But outside this chain-link fence, he rebelled by stealing food. By getting into fights.

"What happened?"

"Got caught," he said. "Cops arrested me. I called Mom to get me out of jail. On the way to pick me up, she got pulled over. She was drunk so we both spent the night in jail. It never would have happened if I'd just stayed home."

"She was drunk. She was driving drunk." I gaped at him as my temper bubbled. "Drunk drivers *murder* innocent people, Karson."

"I know that. Don't you think I know that?" His voice

cracked. "She could have killed someone else's parents and it would have been my fault."

"No, it would have been her fault."

He shook his head. "Mine, Clara. I fucked up. And it wasn't the first or last time."

"What else happened?"

"Fights, mostly. Got suspended from school three times. I beat the shit out of one of her boyfriends with a baseball bat because he tried to have sex with her when she was practically unconscious. Turns out, she didn't care. When she sobered up, it was my fault that he left her. He had money too. He'd been paying for our food. And I chased him away. We didn't eat for a week. I never asked how she finally got money. My guess is she went out and found a new guy. I did that. I made her whore herself out because I couldn't control my temper."

Was he even listening to his own words? "You were trying to protect her."

"She didn't see it that way."

"You can't be serious." His mother was a bitch. She could have gotten a job. She could have provided for her son instead of blaming him for her problems.

Karson shrugged. "After sixteen years of her reminding me every damn day that I was worthless, of her telling me that I'd ruined her life, I decided it was enough. If I was ruining her life, why stay?"

Oh, God. My heart cracked. He was so good. So incredible. How could his own mother not see that?

How could he have this so wrong? "No, Karson. It's not you."

"She loved my father. Maybe the only person in her life that she actually loved more than herself. I don't think she was a drunk back then. But he split two weeks after I was born."

"That's not your fault." He'd been born to shitty parents.

"It is and it isn't. That's just my life."

"Karson, you did not ruin her life."

He didn't say a word.

He didn't believe me.

"Karson. That's not on you."

Again, silence. No matter what I said, he didn't see it. Why? How? There was no way he should carry all of this on his shoulders. "You really think you ruined her life."

He looked up and the raw honesty in his eyes broke my heart. "I think we ruined each other. I think there are toxic people in this world and maybe I'm one of them."

"You're not," I insisted, clenching my jaw so I wouldn't scream. "You're not toxic."

"I was for her. And maybe others."

He didn't mean me, did he? He couldn't. No way. Karson was the foundation to our lives here. He'd been there for all of us.

"I don't know what to say," I whispered.

He shrugged. "Nothing to say."

"I'm sorry." Yes, Craig had been a nightmare, but our

parents had loved us. That was the one thing Aria and I had always held tight to. Our parents had loved us.

It set us apart from the others in the junkyard.

No matter how many times I saw it, how many of my friends had gone through it, I still couldn't understand how a mother or father couldn't love their children.

"She's wrong." I twisted my hand and threaded my fingers through Karson's. "You have to know that. She's so wrong. You're amazing. You're the best guy I've ever known."

He stared at our fingers but didn't reply.

"Karson."

No response.

He didn't believe me. I could sit here and scream it into his face, but he was not hearing my words. Whatever that bitch of a mother had done to him had slashed deep. He covered it up with that dreamy smile and easy charm, but there were wounds hidden beneath.

"Why did she go to the cops?" I asked. "Why would she bring them to the car wash?"

"Desperation? Before I ran away, I stole a bunch of jewelry from her. I pawned it ages ago, but maybe she thinks I still have it. That she can blackmail me into coming home. Who knows? She's crazy, remember?"

"It's not like they can do anything to you. They can't prove you pawned it, though, can they?"

"Maybe. That was a long time ago but . . . they'll

believe her over me," he muttered. "They'll want to know where I'm living and search my things."

"Can they do that?"

"They're the cops."

And if they came here, we were in trouble. "Lou wouldn't let them in."

"He won't have a choice."

"Why would she think that getting the cops involved would make you go home? Or talk to her?"

He circled a finger around his temple. "You're thinking rationally now. Nothing she does is rational. But she can cry on cue. She'll give you these eyes that make you feel bad for her. It's all a trap. She needs money and at first, she must have thought she could guilt me into being her meal ticket. Now she's going for blackmail."

And she seemed determined. His mother would come here eventually. Of that, I had no doubt. She'd find a way to torment him until . . .

Until he was gone.

My heart ached. I knew what I had to say, and I knew the words would taste like acid on my tongue. "You should go. Leave early. Start exploring the world and live your life."

Karson's gaze met mine and softened, then he let go of my hand to cup my cheek. "I'm not ready to leave you yet."

I leaned into his touch as my heart flipped. "I'm not ready either."

Not when I'd just found him. There was so little time left. I didn't want to cut it short.

A muted curse came from beyond the tent's walls. Karson pulled his hand away and I inched backward, putting space between us, right before Aria poked her head inside. "I stubbed my toe."

"No shower?"

She lifted the soap, towel and washcloth in her hand. "I decided to water my plants again first. It was hot today. And I was just thinking that maybe we should tell Lou. Warn him about your mom and the cops."

"Yeah," Karson mumbled. "Probably a good idea. I'll tell him in the morning. He's better in the mornings."

Lou rarely came outside in the afternoons or evenings. It was something I hadn't noticed for a long time, not until Gemma had pointed it out.

"Okay. I'm dealing with the stink that is me," Aria said.

"I'm going to hang out here for a while."

She nodded, then left us alone with a wave.

I turned to Karson, waiting until her footsteps disappeared. Then he was there, kissing me. His hands framed my face and his lips consumed mine. I melted into him, shifting closer to wrap my arms around his waist.

God, I wasn't ready to say goodbye.

I wanted time. I wanted more kisses. I wanted . . . Karson. I wanted him to be the one.

A whimper escaped my throat as Karson dragged his

lips away. I opened my eyes to find his hazel irises waiting and full of lust.

"Did you tell Aria?"

I shook my head, breathing, "No. I wasn't sure what we were."

"I get it." He dropped his forehead to mine. "We'd better slow down."

"Yeah," I muttered.

Aria would know if I showed up at the truck with swollen lips and flushed cheeks. I loved my sister, but Karson was mine, and I didn't want to share. Just this one thing I wanted as my own.

I didn't want to hear her warnings. I didn't want to answer her questions.

How long? What about Londyn? Do you love him?

"I better go," I breathed.

He nodded and let me go, his Adam's apple bobbing as he swallowed. If there were time, if I were braver, I'd lick the column of that throat. I'd taste the saltiness of his skin, like so many of the characters did in my books.

I stood and walked to the doorway on shaky legs. Walking away from Karson was like waking from a dream. I longed to go back, to kiss him again. Because with him, I could get lost in another world. A world without junkyards and dead parents and peanut butter and honey sandwiches.

How was I supposed to leave him for Las Vegas? How

was I supposed to walk away from the only person who could make reality disappear?

I couldn't. He had to come with us. If he tried Vegas, he might like it.

"Karson—"

"Come back tonight."

We spoke in unison.

"Okay," I agreed. Tonight, I'd ask him again tonight. I'd beg if I had to. But he had to come with us.

With my fingertips pressed to my lips, I returned to the truck, where I sat on my bed and did my best to look normal by the time Aria arrived from her shower. Then we busied ourselves by dividing up the books, each deciding which three we'd bring along.

I loved time with my sister, but every minute dragged until finally, she yawned as darkness crept over the junkyard.

"I'm going to bed."

A wave of excitement stirred in my belly. "Oh. Already? I'm not tired."

She stripped off her jeans and pulled on the ratty sleep shorts she'd had for years. It was a good thing neither of us had bloomed early. Though my pants were snug in the hips and shirts stretched across my breasts, our bodies hadn't changed so much that we'd had to buy completely new clothes over the years.

But someday. Someday I would wear clothing without a single tear or frayed hem.

"Are you going to read?" She yawned again as she climbed into her sleeping bag.

"Actually, I might see if Karson wants to play cards or something. We were in a poker game last night."

"Okay." She snuggled with her pillow.

"I'll close this door. In case I just crash there again. In Katherine's room." Before Aria could say anything else, I scurried from the truck, closing the back so she was safe inside.

Karson was outside the tent, standing with his face turned toward the stars.

"Hey," I said, slowing my footsteps even though my heart was pounding.

He looked down and the wide smile he gave me caused tingles to skate across my skin. "Hey."

"What are you looking at?" I searched the sky but there weren't many stars out yet.

"Nothing. Just waiting for you."

"So, um, what do you want to do? Play cards?"

He shook his head.

"Talk?"

He shook his head again, and in one stride he was in my space. His hands came to my face, tilting my chin so he could smash his lips on mine.

I let out a mewl as his arms banded around me, pulling me flush against the hard lines of his tall body. Then he swept me off my feet, my toes skimming across the dirt as he carried me to the tent.

Karson ducked inside, breaking away from my mouth, but his arms never loosened their hold until we were both on our knees in the center of the room.

Our lips were fused together. Our tongues glided and stroked and dived in for more. His hands skimmed over my ribs and down my hips. Then he cupped my breasts and the intimate touch startled a gasp.

"You okay?"

I nodded. "Yeah."

"Did I go too far?"

"No." I leaned into his touch, my nipples hardening. "It's okay."

But even with the assurance, Karson pulled his hands away. He inched backward on his knees. "We'd better slow down."

"Oh." The disappointment in my tone filled the space.

"I don't want to rush this."

"We only have two days left."

"Clara, I want you. God, I want you. But . . ." He ran a hand over his jaw. "Maybe you should go."

Because he wouldn't want to stop.

I didn't want him to stop.

Maybe if my life had been normal. If I were the girl who'd crushed on the boy in school. If we had had weeks of flirting beside lockers and going on dates, then I would have slowed this down.

But we only had two days. And if I couldn't convince him to come to Vegas, then I'd lose him.

"I don't want to go." I squared my shoulders, feigning more confidence than I actually felt.

Karson let out a pained groan. "Clara."

"I want you to be the one," I whispered.

His eyes locked on mine and whatever restraint he'd been holding onto shredded. He came at me, strong and sure, and kissed me until I was breathless. Then he took me to his room, laying me on the bed that I'd slept on with him just last night.

Karson's kisses were tender and soft as he settled on his side, careful not to crush me under his weight. "Tell me to stop and I'll stop."

"Don't stop." I closed my eyes and arched into his lips as they trailed down my neck.

One of his hands was on my breast, the other in my hair.

When his fingers drifted to the waistband of my jeans, I ached in places I hadn't ached before. A throb boomed in my core.

Karson never pushed too fast. He looked at me before every touch, waiting for that nod to continue. He let me conquer the fears, one by one. He let me know with his kiss and his touch and those gorgeous hazel eyes that I was in control.

And when we were both naked, our clothes piled beside us, he settled into the cradle of my hips and brushed his thumb across my cheek.

"Clara." He whispered my name like a prayer.

I ran my fingers across his collarbone. I fit my palm to the hard muscle of his bicep. Then I gave him the nod that brought us together as one.

Later, after he'd made me see a different kind of stars, we curled together, our legs tangled and his arms encircling mine. I fell asleep with a smile.

Karson didn't know it, but he'd just given me something I'd never had before.

A dream come true.

CHAPTER EIGHT

CLARA

The murmur of voices woke me from sleep. "Who is tha—"

"Shh." Karson's arms squeezed around me as he whispered in my ear. Then he let me go and silently slipped from beneath his blankets, swiping up his jeans from the floor. He tugged them on and tiptoed, barefoot, toward the opening of the tent. With a glance over his shoulder, he pressed a finger to his lips and crept outside.

I scrambled to get dressed, strapping on my bra first, then rifling through the clothes scattered around me for my panties. With them on, I yanked on my jeans and shirt, then followed Karson outside. Crouching low as I walked, I weaved through the piles of junk around the tent, finding him ducked behind an old truck.

Aria was by his side.

They were both staring at Lou, who stood beside the gate.

Talking to two police officers.

Their voices echoed across the yard.

Lou's was gruff and raspy as he thrust a photo back at one of the cops. "Never seen him."

"Are you sure?" The officer took the photo, looking at it himself. "This is an outdated photo. Maybe you could look again."

Lou scowled. "Never seen that kid."

The officers shared a look. "Sir, we have reason to believe this young man is living here. In your junkyard. On your property."

"Not here."

"Mr. Miley, if we could just take a look around—"

"No," Lou barked. "There's no kid here. Don't you think I'd know if a damn kid was living at my place?"

"There are a lot of places where a person could hide." One officer scanned the junkyard. When his face shifted our way, all three of us hit the dirt.

Aria's face was pale. She sat unmoving other than the short, fast breaths that made her chest rise and fall. They matched mine.

Karson's jaw was clenched tight and his fists balled at his sides.

His mother had done this. She'd sent the police here and given them that photo.

"There's no one here but me," Lou repeated, agitation tainting his words.

Maybe I heard the lie because I knew the truth. But if I didn't believe Lou, the cops might not either.

"We believe he's involved in a breaking and entering," one of the officers said. "He's been stealing from his mother for years now. Family heirlooms and such. She's finally decided to get the authorities involved."

"Fuck," Karson muttered.

So his mother had decided to blackmail him.

The three of us shifted again, daring another glance at the officers. Thankfully, neither was looking our way. They were focused on Lou, who seemed to be getting more frazzled every second. He shifted his weight from foot to foot. He rattled the ring of keys in his hand.

Even when he had customers come to the yard, he'd point them in the right direction, then send them on their way. He never played tour guide. If a mechanic or antique hunter came here searching for spare parts, they were left on their own, given clear directions where they could and could not search. And Lou never haggled. He had signs around the shack saying as much.

It was all so he didn't have to prolong human interaction.

"Would you call us if you see anyone?" one of the officers asked, handing over a card.

Lou nodded and took the paper, shoving it into the

pocket of his baggy jeans. Then, without waiting for the cops to leave, he turned and disappeared into his shack, slamming the door behind him.

The officers shared a look of disbelief, then walked to the street, where their cruiser was parked. As they rolled down the road, Karson, Aria and I stayed hidden, waiting until the only sound was the soft breeze through the drying summer grasses around the property.

Karson was the first to stand, shaking his head as he marched to the tent.

Aria stood and sighed. "Shit."

"This is bad." I got to my bare feet and pinched the bridge of my nose. "This is very bad. He told me a little about her last night. His mother. From the sound of it, she's a manipulative, lying bitch."

"He should leave."

The twist in my chest was so tight I struggled to breathe. She was right. The best thing was for Karson to move on. But I wasn't ready to give him up. Not yet. Not after last night.

"You slept in the tent again," she said.

"We played cards pretty late. I didn't want to wake you," I lied.

Today was not the day to tell Aria I'd given Karson my virginity.

The sound of a slamming door echoed across the yard. Aria and I both turned toward the shop door, recognizing the sound.

Karson had disappeared to the bathroom.

"I'm going to go get my shoes." I left Aria's side and hurried to the tent, scanning around Karson's bed for anything I might have left behind. Only my shoes and socks remained. The condom he'd worn last night was gone, along with the wrapper.

I blushed and took a moment to breathe before I had to face my sister again.

Should I tell her? It would make it all easier if she knew what had happened, right? There'd be no sneaking around. Right. I'd just tell her. Decision made, I stepped into my shoes and found her in the truck. I climbed inside as she was making her bed.

"I, um . . ." *Tell her.*

The words clogged my throat.

Why was I so scared to confess that I'd been with Karson? I was in love with him. People in love had sex. But I couldn't get my mouth to form the sentence.

"Um, what?"

"Nothing." I swallowed hard. "Once Karson is done, I'm going to take a shower too. Then we should talk."

"I'm just glad I showered before the cops showed up." She plopped down on her bed. "They totally would have seen me coming out of the shop."

"Maybe we should start showering at night."

"Maybe." Her gaze was focused on the truck wall, her forehead furrowed. She was staring at today's number.

One.

It wouldn't matter when we showered because today was our last day.

Tonight was our last night.

The urge to cry came on so strong I almost dropped to my knees.

The shop door slammed again, this time not as loud. I blinked the tears away and collected my soap and towel, then went to the shop, finally breathing when I was under the warm spray.

I hated the idea of washing away Karson's kisses. His touches. My body was sore in places I'd never been sore before, and the tenderness between my legs was going to make work difficult today. It was my last shift at the diner.

Still, despite the ache, a smile toyed at my lips as I toweled off.

Karson and I had had sex. We'd been as intimate as two people could get.

Would he change his mind about Vegas now? Did he feel the same way about me that I felt about him?

Dressed in fresh clothes and smelling like my soap, I hurried to the truck, finding Karson already there, waiting with Aria.

"Hey." I gave him a tiny smile.

With his back to Aria, he winked at me. "Hey."

"So what do we do?" Aria hopped out of the truck to pace beside her buckets of plants.

Karson dropped to the truck's edge, sitting so his legs could hang over the end.

And I took the space by his side, careful not to get too close. What I wanted to do was pull him aside, to see if we were okay. To let him kiss me again. But not until we talked.

"I don't understand why she's doing this," I said. "Your mom. Why couldn't she just let you go? You ran away. You're done with her."

Karson scoffed. "Like I told you last night. She's crazy and desperate. Her life's mission is to make mine hell."

"I hate her," I spat, fury racing through my veins.

"Join the club," he mumbled. "She won't stop. And I don't like that look the cops had when they left. I think they knew Lou was lying."

"If they come here again, they'll find us." Aria waved to our home. "Three teenagers are sort of hard to miss."

Karson nodded and turned to face me. *No.* The look in his eyes made me want to scream.

I knew before he opened his mouth what he was going to say. "We're leaving tomorrow anyway."

"Yeah." Aria ran her hands over a pink bloom from a bucket. "We'll be gone first thing in the morning."

My heart was breaking.

This had always been the plan. Always.

"Come with us." My plea escaped before I could stop it. "You could come with us."

The look Karson gave me was so gentle and kind, I wanted to die.

Because in that look was his answer.

No. He wouldn't come to Vegas with us.

"It's okay." I waved it off so he wouldn't have to come up with an explanation.

"Clara."

"It was just an idea." I got to my feet and went into the truck, folding up the clothes I'd worn last night. They were trash. I'd leave them behind. Still, I folded.

"What time are you going to work?" Aria joined me in the truck.

I glanced at my little clock. "I'd better leave soon."

When I turned to Karson, he was staring at the number on the truck's wall.

One.

Time was up. We'd just started this. And now it was ending.

Without so much as a glance in my direction, Karson jumped down and vanished.

I wanted to cry. I wanted to yell. I wanted to beg him not to leave us.

Instead, I blinked away the threat of tears.

And went to work.

"HEY." Karson knocked on the side of the truck.

I tensed as he hopped inside. "Hey."

"How's it going? It looks different in here."

"Yeah."

After my shift had ended, Aria and I had spent the afternoon and early evening organizing. The items that were coming with us were stowed in our backpacks, ready for tomorrow. Everything else we'd moved to the front of the truck. The bedding. The books. The clothes. The forgotten pieces that would probably remain in this truck until the end of the junkyard's days.

"Where's Aria?" he asked.

"Moving her plants. She's staging them beside Lou's."

"Does she need help?"

I shook my head. "I think she wanted to be alone for a while. She was going to write him a note."

"Clara, about Vegas."

"You don't have to explain. I get it. You've done your duty and stayed to watch us. You don't deserve to be chained to us anymore."

"Is that how you think I feel? Chained?"

I lifted a shoulder. "I wouldn't blame you if you did."

"Well, I don't."

"Then why?" I asked even though I knew the answer. My voice was too loud and it bounced off the metal walls.

The emotion was bubbling up and I was about to lose it, so I gave him my back, not wanting him to see me cry. I'd had to take three breaks from the dishwasher today to run to the bathroom and cry. When my boss had given me my final pay, I think she'd thought the tears in my eyes had been because I was leaving.

"Because you shouldn't be chained *to me*." His hand

came to my shoulder and his thumb circled the bare skin of my neck. "Would you look at me?"

"I can't." My voice cracked.

"Clara, you deserve this fresh start. I won't risk ruining it for you. What if I got caught stealing? What if I got into another fight? What if someone asked when we started having sex and then I got put away for statutory rape?"

My hands fisted at my sides. He could stop stealing. He could stop fighting. "I would never tell."

"I'm not going to make you lie for me. I won't ruin you too."

"You wouldn't."

"I might. I don't want to take that chance."

My throat burned. "Even for me?"

"Especially for you. We all deserve to be set free."

Yes, he did. Karson deserved to be set free.

No matter what I said, he truly thought of himself as a toxic person. Maybe if I'd seen it sooner, years ago, I could have convinced him of the truth. But after weeks, I couldn't even persuade him to go exploring with me in Vegas. How was I supposed to convince him that he was not the person his mother had spent sixteen years telling him he was?

I didn't have sixteen years to fix this. I only had a day.

It was too late. I was too late.

Tears flooded my eyes as I spun around to face him. I'd worked so hard today to keep them at bay and hide my emotions from my coworkers and Aria. But there was no hiding from Karson, not anymore.

He stepped closer and caught the first tear as it dropped down my cheek. "Don't cry."

"I don't want to say goodbye."

"Then we won't."

A sob escaped right as he pulled me into his arms, holding me close as I cried. More footsteps sounded in the truck and when one of Karson's arms loosened, it was only to make room for Aria to join our huddle.

The three of us clung to one another, and when Karson finally let us go, my tears had soaked his shirt and Aria was sniffling.

"Where will you go?" she asked him.

"Exploring," Karson and I answered in unison, then laughed.

"Out of Temecula, that's for sure," he said, then looked to me. "And maybe someday, to visit you two in Vegas. I expect you'll be running the town by then."

I forced a smile. "That's the plan."

"What time are you leaving?" Aria asked.

"Early. You?"

"We'll go to the bus station first thing," I said. "The bus to Vegas leaves at nine. But we'll be early, just in case."

"So this is it. The last night. Calls for a celebration."

"Like what?" I followed him as he walked to the end of the truck to look out at the junkyard.

"Peanut butter and honey sandwiches, of course."

HOURS LATER, after the sun had set and Aria had fallen asleep, I snuck out of the truck, careful not to wake her, and I made my way to the tent.

Karson's lantern was on. His bags were packed beside the door and he was sitting on his bed.

Waiting for me.

Neither of us spoke as he took me in his arms and kissed me breathless. Or as he stripped off my clothes and his own. Or as he made love to me, one last time, holding me tight until morning.

I refused to fall asleep when he drifted off. Instead, I clung to him until the first rays of dawn lit the sky, and I snuck to the shop for a shower before he or Aria woke up.

While Aria was in the bathroom, I found the small notebook and pen Aria kept in her pack and tore out a page. Then I wrote Lou a note, leaving it at the base of his front door.

I LOVE YOU, *Lou. Thank you.*
    Clara

. . .

"GOODBYE, LOU," I whispered to his shack. "Take care of yourself."

Aria had done her farewell yesterday. Never before had her plants looked so green and her flowers so bold as they did around his shack. She'd staged them so artfully, I doubted even a professional gardener would have done such a nice job.

While she collected her things, I set out a bowl of cat food for Katherine's cat. Then I took the half-empty bag of food to the shop, leaving it beside the door where Lou would find it.

"I didn't think I'd be sad," Aria said as we both stood outside the truck.

I had. I'd known this would hurt.

We each wore a backpack on our shoulders and held another in our hands. On the wall, I'd erased yesterday's number, but I hadn't written anything in its place.

"Thank you," I said to the truck, my chin quivering. *Thank you for being our home. Thank you for being our refuge. Thank you for keeping us safe.*

With tears in my eyes, I took Aria's hand. Then, like the day we'd come here, we walked, together, toward the gate.

I didn't look at the Cadillac. I didn't look at the tent.

I knew it would be empty.

I kept my face forward and my feet moving until we journeyed down our road one last time. Until we were at the station with bus tickets in our pockets. And as I settled into my seat on the bus that would take us to Vegas, I replayed the last words we'd said to each other before he'd fallen asleep.

"*Happy Birthday, Clara.*"
"*Will I ever see you again?*"
"*I hope so. I really hope so.*"

CHAPTER NINE

KARSON

T*welve years later . . .*
"It's really you."
Clara Saint-James.

There she was, standing in my driveway, and all I could do was grin at her like a fool. She looked beautiful. More beautiful than I'd ever imagined.

"It's really me." She smiled and my heart fluttered. Her smile had always hit me dead center.

The boy at her side stared up at me. Other than a quick glance, I hadn't paid him much attention, because it was impossible to tear my eyes away from Clara for long.

God, I'd imagined this. I'd hoped for this. Just to see her again, in the flesh, and know that she was safe. Know that she'd found a new life. Know that she was happy.

"What are you doing here?"

"It's a long story." She waved a hand toward her car.

I followed the movement, taking in the classic Cadillac. It was a stunner, but nothing like Clara. The hood ornament, a V embossed with red and gold and silver, glinted under the sun. It looked familiar. Too familiar.

I knew that ornament.

I knew that car.

"Wait. Is this . . ."

Clara nodded. "Looks a little different than it did back in the day, huh?"

"What? How?" My jaw dropped as I rushed to the car, splaying my hands on the cherry-red hood, the metal still warm. I walked along the Cadillac's side, inspecting and savoring every inch. "I can't believe it. I can't believe this is the same car. It's incredible."

The Cadillac was a dream. It looked nothing like the rusted heap it had been so many years ago. The interior was refinished in a white, soft leather. The dash, which had been cracked and busted, was new. The polished chrome accents sparkled.

I had no idea what had brought this car and Clara to California, but what a Sunday surprise.

Skimming my fingers over a rear fin that bordered the broad trunk, I touched the car again just to prove it was real. "I bet I won't find peanut butter and honey stashed in here like we used to."

She scoffed. "Most definitely not."

"How?" Clara was the best of this surprise visit, but the car was the literal red cherry on top.

"Londyn," she said.

"Londyn." I nodded, rounding the trunk. "Before Lou died, he told me that she'd called and bought the car. But I didn't expect to see it again. How do you have it?"

"Kind of a long story." She looked down at the boy and smiled. "We surprised you today. Want to meet for dinner or something? If you're free?"

"I'm free now." There was no way I was letting her out of my sight. Not yet. I glanced down at the boy who watched my every step as I approached. I crouched down in front of him and held out a hand for a shake. "But how about some introductions first? I'm Karson. What's your name?"

"August." He looked at my hand, then slapped his to mine, grabbing it tighter than I would have expected for a young kid. One hard shake and he looked up at Clara and smiled.

She winked down at him.

"Quite a grip." I shook out my hand, pretending it hurt. "You're pretty strong for a—what, four-year-old?"

"I'm five. Almost six."

"Ah. Still, you're pretty strong." I grinned at him as he puffed up his chest, then stood and motioned toward my home. "Did you ever learn to like coffee?"

"I can't believe you remember that." Clara's pretty brown eyes softened, and I was whisked away to the past. To a junkyard where I'd once fallen for a girl with pretty brown eyes. This girl.

"Coffee became a necessity because of this guy." Clara ruffled August's hair. "He loves to torment his mother in the middle of the night."

"Nu-uh," he argued.

"Yes-huh."

His mother. Clara was a mother. I'd already known. One look at them and it was no secret. The resemblance, along with the onslaught of surprises in the past five minutes, was enough to keep my head spinning.

The boy looked just like her. They had the same mouth and nose. They had the same sparkling eyes with flecks of gold. His hair was the color of honey, like hers was in my memory.

A twist pinched in my gut. Clara was a mother. Where was the father? Why hadn't he come along? I had no right to be jealous, but as sure as a Cadillac from over a decade ago was parked in my driveway, envy took up the free space in my chest.

My eyes flew to her left hand. Other than the stack of bracelets on her wrist, there was no other jewelry. Was she divorced then?

Maybe if I stopped gawking at her and invited her inside, she'd answer those questions.

"Coffee." I cleared my throat and extended a hand toward the house.

"Want to grab your Nintendo?" Clara asked August.

He answered by sprinting to the car and vaulting over

the side wall for the seat in the back, rifling through a bag. He emerged with a handheld game and a smile.

They had the same smile too. Bright. Cheerful. Honest.

"God, it's good to see you." The words spilled out.

A flush crept into her cheeks. "I wasn't sure you'd remember me."

"What?"

"It was a long time ago."

"It could have been fifty years. A hundred. I will always know you."

Clara swallowed hard and pressed a hand to her heart. "It's good to see you too."

Bubbly music chimed between us. August was already playing his game, concentration scrunching his face.

"Come on in." I jerked my chin for the house.

"Hit pause, bud," Clara said, then gripped August's hand as they followed me to the door. "This is a beautiful home."

"Thanks. I got it for a steal." A three-million-dollar steal. Homes in this neighborhood of Elyria didn't come cheap. I walked to the living room, gesturing to the caramel leather couches. "Make yourself at home. I'll get coffee. And for August?"

"Water's fine," Clara said, taking a seat on the love seat.

August plopped down beside her, his thumbs on the

Nintendo's controllers and his eyes glued to the game as the music started up again.

"Ever wish we'd had those things?"

Clara laughed. "Then I would have had another game to beat you at."

"Please." I scoffed. "I let you win, remember?"

"I remember too." Her smile turned bittersweet.

"Be back." I disappeared into the kitchen and took a moment to collect myself.

Holy fuck. That was not who I'd expected to see in the driveway today. And with that car. And alone with her son.

Clara Saint-James.

My Clara.

She hadn't been mine for a long time. My mind acknowledged that truth. But in my heart . . . she'd always felt like mine.

I shook my head, focusing on the coffee pot. I'd brewed a large pot today because I'd slept like shit last night. Though I always slept like shit. Waking at three or four in the morning had become normal over the past decade. If I got five hours sleep, that was a good night.

There was just too much on my mind. Too much to shut down.

Too many thoughts.

Clara was one of them.

How had she found me? How had Londyn's car found its way to Clara? And what about the others? Had she heard from them? The questions seemed endless. I swiped a bottle of water from the fridge and carried the coffee mugs to the living room.

Clara was bent over her son, watching along as he played with more animation than the game characters themselves.

"Here you go." I handed her a mug, then took the couch opposite hers, setting my coffee on a coaster so it could cool.

"Thanks." She did the same, then touched some buttons on August's game, turning the volume down.

He shot her a scowl but didn't argue.

"Your home is gorgeous," she said, taking in the room's white walls and plethora of windows.

"I wanted something bright. Airy. I like to be able to see outside."

"Mine's got more of a modern style, but lots of windows too."

"Where do you live?"

"Welcome, Arizona. It's a little town on old Route 66. I moved there five years ago, when August was a baby." She toyed with his hair, brushing it off his forehead as he played.

"You like it there?"

She nodded. "I do. It's quiet and safe. Good schools. The desert is truly beautiful in the spring, when the wildflowers bloom. Though at the moment, it's hot. Aria just moved there."

"Aria." I smiled at the name. A name I hadn't said aloud for years. I hadn't spoken any of their names in longer than I could remember. "How is she?"

"Great. She just had a baby. She's married to my boss, Brody. They live next door so we can invade each other's privacy on a regular basis."

"Good for her." I leaned forward and put my elbows to my knees. "Okay, I was going to go for small talk, but the curiosity is killing me. How are you here?"

She stretched for her coffee mug. "Like I said. Londyn. That's the short answer."

"Londyn." Another name. Another memory. "I'm going to need more than that."

Clara laughed and shifted in her seat, crossing a leg over the other. She moved with such elegance. It was something I'd always noticed. She was graceful, like a dancer who'd missed out on dance lessons, but the talent didn't need instruction because it was in her bones. If anything, time seemed to have only accentuated her poise.

"Londyn hauled the car to Boston and had it restored," she said.

"But she didn't keep it?"

Clara shook her head. "She wants you to have it."

"Me?" My jaw hit the area rug beneath the couch. "Seriously? Why?"

"Because it was yours too. That was the reason she gave me. But I think because she doesn't need it anymore. She found what she was looking for."

"Is she happy?"

Clara smiled. "She is. She lives in West Virginia with her husband. Has a couple of cute little kids."

Something inside me clicked. A piece snapped into place. A worry disappeared. For many, many years I'd wondered what had happened to Londyn. To Clara. To the rest of our junkyard crew. I hadn't had the courage to seek them out. Maybe I'd been too afraid of what I'd find. But knowing Londyn was happy was a balm to the soul.

"Good. You've seen her?"

"Just on our virtual chats. We have them every month or so. It started as a book club but we rarely discuss books. Mostly we talk. Catch up on the years we missed. The chats are a fairly recent thing. Ever since the Cadillac started its trip across the country."

Another string of questions zipped through my mind but rather than blurt them in rapid succession, I picked up my coffee and settled into the couch. "I think you'd better give me the long answer now."

She laughed. "We might need more coffee."

"For you? I'll make all the pots in the world. I also have lemonade with lots and lots of ice."

"You remember that too?"

Everything. "I remember everything."

———

AN HOUR LATER, I stared at Clara in amazement. There was no other word for her story. It was simply amazing.

"Handoffs. That's . . . damn, that's cool."

"Right?" She'd been smiling for nearly the entire hour we'd talked. With every twist and turn of the Cadillac's journey across the country, her smile seemed to widen.

And I kept on drowning, sinking deeper and deeper into those twinkling eyes and breathtaking smile.

"So Londyn's in West Virginia," I said. "Gemma and Kat in Montana. And you and Aria in Arizona."

"Yep." She nodded. "I don't know if we would have come together again without that Cadillac. Maybe. I guess I like to hope so. But it's been the catalyst. All because Londyn wants you to have it."

"But I can't take it." I shook my head. "That car must have cost her a small fortune."

"She doesn't care about the money. She wants you to have it. You deserve that car. You were the one who made it safe for us to live at Lou's. You stayed. You protected us."

"It's too much."

"No, it's not enough." She shook her head. "Besides, I'm not taking it with me when we go home. And after you spend an hour or two behind the wheel, you'll never let it go."

I chuckled. "Should we go for a drive?"

"I was hoping you'd say that." Clara nudged August away from the game. "Gus, time for a break."

"Okay, Mom." He looked up at her with so much love and admiration. That kid worshiped his mother. *Lucky guy.* All kids deserved to have a mother like Clara.

We hadn't gotten into much of her story yet. Or his. I hoped we would on the drive because while my curiosity was sated for the moment, the hunger to know everything about her would return.

I stood from the couch and collected her empty coffee mug. We'd been so into the story, I hadn't needed a refill. I'd been glued to her every word. "Let me put these in the sink. I'll meet you outside."

With flip-flops on my feet and my wallet tucked into a pocket of my shorts, I found them in the driveway. August was already buckled into his car seat while Clara stood beside the passenger door. Her green shorts left her long, tanned legs on display. A white tee draped over her trim frame.

Beautiful. She'd only grown more beautiful.

She tossed me the keys with a smirk and popped open her door.

It was strange, getting behind the wheel of a car I'd once slept in for months. One glance at the backseat and I didn't see white leather or August, but Londyn lounging against one side while I was against the other, our legs tangled.

Clara followed my gaze. "It's hard not to see her back there, isn't it?"

"We had a lot of good times in this car."

"What's that saying? You never forget your first love."

My gaze shifted to her face.

Londyn hadn't been mine. I was sure that Clara thought so, but Londyn had been a great girlfriend. A best friend. My first love? No. I'd thought so at the time but now, years later, after growing up, I knew the difference between affection and love.

"No, you don't forget."

When she turned my way, something crossed her face. Shock, maybe. Or was she back there with me, at the junkyard when we'd lain on the hood of this car to count shooting stars?

"Where are we going?" August asked.

I tore my eyes away from Clara's soft lips and put the key into the ignition.

Clara cleared her throat. "Um, just for a drive."

"Another drive," he groaned. "For how long?"

"Short." I turned and gave him a wink. "Promise."

"I bet we could drive by the ocean again," Clara said.

"Sure thing." I started the engine, feeling the rumble and vibration of what had to be a state-of-the-art engine. "Ahh. She purrs. Like she always should have."

"And she floats." Clara dug a pair of sunglasses from her purse and slid them on, covering up those sparkling irises.

I fought the urge to take them from her face. I fought the swell in my chest—and behind my zipper.

Get your shit together, Avery. This should not be my

reaction. It had to be history, right? Shock? That was the only explanation for why my head and my body were having such a hard time distinguishing the Clara from my memory and the Clara riding shotgun.

Shaking it off, I put the Cadillac in reverse and backed out of the driveway. I drove us to the highway, and as my foot pressed the gas pedal, I couldn't help but smile. "Oh, yeah, she floats."

"Told you."

"Londyn's never getting this car back."

Clara giggled. "She thought you might say that."

"I feel like an asshole for not keeping in touch." Though I'd had my reasons. Or excuses.

"He said a bad word." August sat up straight in his seat, but instead of a glare or scowl, he was grinning eagerly.

"Sorry." I gave Clara an exaggerated frown.

"You owe him a quarter. He's going to fund his college tuition off the bad language of the adults in his life, aren't you, Gus?"

"Yep. I have three hundred twenty-seven dollars and fifty cents."

"Wow." I shifted in my seat, keeping one hand on the wheel so I could dig my wallet out of my shorts pocket with the other. By some miracle, there were three quarters inside the main fold. I plucked them out and passed them all back. "This is in case you bust me later today."

"That's what Uncle Brody does too. He calls it paying in advance."

"Brody has supplied the bulk of that three hundred and twenty-seven dollars," Clara said.

We drove for a few miles, letting the wind blow past us, but curiosity kept gnawing at me.

Where was August's father? Why didn't Clara have a ring on her finger? Had they met in Vegas? How long had she worked there? Why had she left? When?

Damn it, I shouldn't have looked her up all those years ago. One ten-minute glimpse into her life on Facebook, and I'd been haunted by a string of pictures ever since. Those photos had taken on a life of their own in my imagination. I'd seen her with him. I'd seen her happy and free.

I'd lived with them and the envy that tainted them because in my mind, Clara had been happy. She was happy, right? She looked happy. So why were she and August here alone?

Maybe I shouldn't have let those pictures scare me away.

I glanced at Clara, memorizing the small smile on her mouth. Not that I needed to. I'd memorized that look years ago. August's attention was rapt on the passing buildings and the ocean beyond.

"Been to the beach yet?" I asked Clara, keeping my voice low.

"Not yet. We came straight to your house."

I grinned at her, then pushed down the blinker and

drove to my favorite spot. When I pulled into the parking lot, August's excitement was palpable. His legs kicked and he bounced in the confines of his seat's harness.

"Can we go swimming?" he asked, nodding like he could influence his mother's answer.

"Uh, not yet. But later we'll go swimming. After we get checked into the hotel."

"How long are you staying?" I unbuckled as she climbed out and helped August out of the car.

"Two nights."

Two nights. Not enough. "What hotel?"

"The Kate Sperry Inn. It's a local spot, I guess." She shrugged. "The ratings were good."

"It's very nice." The place was a four-star hotel that cared more about quality than quantity. She'd have access to the beach and a pool.

"Mom, can I—" He tugged on her arm.

"Go ahead. Only go into the water as far as your ankles." She laughed as he raced away, stumbling a bit on that first footstep into the sand. But he righted himself quickly and threw his arms in the air as he ran.

"I did the exact same thing when I came here." I chuckled and led Clara to the beach. Our pace slowed as we joined August at the water's edge. He dipped a toe in, then dropped to put his hands in the foam.

"I hope you don't feel like we invaded today," she said.

"Not at all. It's a Sunday. I don't do much on Sundays

except come to the beach. Surf if I'm feeling it. Today, I didn't have to come alone."

She tipped her head to the sky, letting the sunshine light the fine contours of her cheeks. Her every movement had my focus. It had always been like that, hadn't it? Even when it shouldn't have been. Even when I'd had to hide it from everyone else.

Clara had always held a special place in my life. She was sweet. She was strong. She made me laugh.

She made me feel like I could move mountains. Like I could swim across the ocean and back. She was . . . she was my Clara.

Maybe that was why it had been so easy to fall for her, even when I'd known I shouldn't.

Twelve years ago. Today. Here I was, still hanging on her every step. Clinging to every word. Every smile.

Even when I knew I shouldn't.

CHAPTER TEN

KARSON

"August loves pizza," Clara said, digging a fork into her salad. "I'll eat it every now and then but rarely."

"Same." I twirled a twist of spaghetti around my fork. "I haven't had peanut butter since."

"Me neither. Gus didn't even know what a peanut butter and jelly sandwich was until he started kindergarten last year. He thinks they are the best things ever."

August was sitting behind a plastic steering wheel with his eyes glued to a video game screen where a race was about to start. The arcade room of the restaurant had been a hit. His foot slammed into the gas pedal and he shifted his body with every turn of the wheel.

After spending the afternoon at the beach, mostly watching August and the ocean, I'd taken them to get checked in to their hotel. Then we'd watched August swim for an hour.

Clara and I had talked poolside, mostly reminiscing about old times. She'd filled me in on the lives of the others and shown me pictures on her phone of Aria and her newborn baby.

The longer the day went on, the more and more I'd resented the noticeable lack of detail about *her* life in our conversation.

So I'd insisted on dinner. I wasn't ready to say goodbye until I knew more of her story.

Around us, the sounds of arcade games filled the air with beeps and bells. Most of the tables were full of parents visiting. Like Clara, they seemed to keep one eye on their children, ready to dole out more quarters when needed.

Garlic and tomato and cheese scents infused the air. The owners of this little Italian restaurant had been brilliant to bring in the games for kids because it brought families here to savor their delicious food. The kids had the games. The parents, the wine selection.

"August is a great kid," I said, smiling as he shot both hands in the air, game won.

"He's my whole world." Clara's eyes lit up when they landed on her son. It reminded me so much of the past. She'd had that same look when we'd stood in line at the movie theater for tickets. Or the day I'd brought her that

GED study guide, even though I'd stolen it. Or when she'd beat me at cards.

When I'd teased her that I'd let her win, when really, she'd kicked my ass.

"I keep getting this feeling like no time at all has passed," I confessed. "Then I blink and remember how long it's been."

"I was thinking the same thing when we were on the beach today. Weird, right?"

"Weird."

Wonderful, heartbreaking, beautiful misery.

I was so damn glad to be sitting across from her. And so fucking sad that I'd missed so much when maybe . . .

Maybe I hadn't had to miss it.

Clara set her fork down and gave me a sad smile. "When you never came to see us in Vegas, I thought maybe . . . oh, never mind."

"Thought what?"

"That you'd forgotten about us. That maybe we weren't as good of friends as I'd built up in my head."

Friends. That word rang through the air like a gunshot. Pain speared my chest. Direct hit.

Was that all she'd thought we were? Friends? Clara had to know that she'd meant so much more. And because of what she'd meant, it was the reason I hadn't gone to Vegas with her in the first place.

I'd had to get my shit together. I'd had to realize that the words she'd once told me were true—that I wasn't toxic to the people in my life. I'd had to grow up. Too bad it'd taken me so damn long.

By then, it had been too late.

"I never forgot about you. You know why I didn't come with you to Vegas after the junkyard. I didn't want to taint your life. I might have run away from my mother, but that didn't mean her words hadn't come to the junkyard with me. It took me a long time to erase them from the back of my mind. To move past them. You were right, what you told me. Wish I had listened. But I needed to figure it out on my own, you know?"

Understanding crossed her face. "Karson."

"It wasn't that I didn't want to go with you. I just didn't want to bring my bullshit into your new life. And by the time I realized it was just that—bullshit—well, a lot of years had passed."

"I get it," she said. "It's the same reason all of us lost touch for so long. We all needed that time to put the past away."

"Exactly."

What I was never good at articulating, Clara could voice perfectly. There was no person on earth who'd gotten me like she always had. She knew it had been my mountain to climb.

God, how I had missed her.

"Thank fuck for that goddamn Cadillac."

She laughed and the sound was a blast to the past. Sweet. Musical. Sincere. Clara's face was like a shooting star when she laughed. You didn't want to blink and miss a second of the show.

A soul-shattering shake ran through my entire body. The same feeling that had come over me years and years ago while I'd been by her side, staring up at the stars from a rusted Cadillac.

I wanted to kiss her. In this moment, I wanted to take her cheeks in my hands and kiss her until I forgot my own name.

Goddamn it. Why? Why now? Why hadn't she come a year ago?

When I was nineteen and after Londyn and I had broken up, I'd known my time with Clara was short. Hell, for the longest time, I hadn't realized she'd liked me that way. I'd done so well at keeping her as a friend and nothing more. Then I'd felt that shake and my willpower had shattered.

That had been the best damn kiss of my life.

But I wasn't nineteen anymore.

Tearing my eyes away, I focused on my food, finishing the last few bites of my pasta. August had decimated his slice of pizza in record time because Clara had promised he could play games but only after eating dinner.

"We've talked so much about the past today," she said, going back to her salad. "I'd like to hear more about you. What do you do for work?"

"I'm a realtor." I put my fork down and found August changing games. This time he was at the Big Game

Hunter. To Clara, it probably looked like I was checking on her kid. Really, I just needed a minute before I faced her again.

I needed to fortify the walls.

Not that it did any damn good. When I turned to her, my heart skipped. So I focused on answering her question. Maybe then she'd answer more of mine.

"I got started about seven years ago. In Temecula, actually."

"I'm surprised you went back."

"For a while." But that was not a story for tonight. "The market was booming, and a friend was working construction for a builder who could barely keep up. The builder had a broker selling all his homes, so I went to work with my friend one day and met the agent. Talked to her for about three hours and decided to get licensed. She sponsored me and I worked for her for a few years. Then I decided to branch out on my own when I moved to Elyria."

"I'm not at all surprised you're successful. Do you like it?"

I nodded. "I do. I work hard. Have some flexibility in my schedule, which I appreciate, and it pays the bills."

"Gemma was in real estate for a while. Before she started her companies and skyrocketed through the stratosphere."

"Sounds like Gemma."

"She hasn't changed." A smile toyed on Clara's pretty mouth. "None of us have, really. We just grew up."

Yes, she'd grown up. And no, she hadn't changed. Thank God for that.

Clara had this ageless wisdom, this realistic vision of the world. She wasn't bitter or harsh or jaded, she just knew that life wasn't fair. And she smiled through it anyway.

"Do you mind that Gemma hired a PI to find you?" she asked.

I shook my head. "Nah. You?"

"No. I'm glad." She collected plates, stacking them and shoving them to the side. Then she rested her forearms on the table with a quick glance at August to make sure his pocket was still bulging with unspent quarters. "Tell me all about exploring."

"Exploring was fun. Really fun." I grinned and draped an arm over the back of my booth.

Clara was still leaning forward, and I ignored the magnetic pull to lean in closer. Clara considered us friends. We were friends. Two old acquaintances swapping stories over a meal. Nothing more.

"I went to LA first. Hated it. Stayed for about a week, then kept going south. Sometimes I hitchhiked. But I walked a lot. Walked until I got to San Diego." The miles had been healing. They'd given me time to reflect and think about where I was going and what I wanted in my life.

At the top of the list had been stability. For that, I'd needed money.

"I stayed in San Diego for about eighteen months. Moved on right before my twenty-first birthday."

"To where?" She propped her chin in a hand, listening. I'd always loved how Clara listened, not just with her ears but her entire body.

"Houston. I stayed there for about three years, working mostly. I took a page from the Clara Saint-James playbook and got my GED."

"I still have that book you gave me. I couldn't throw it out." She smiled. "What did you do there?"

"Worked two jobs, one as a bouncer at a nightclub and another as a caddy at a golf course. I saw a lot of rich people at both places and I decided that I didn't need to be rich, but I sure as hell wasn't going to be poor."

"Amen to that. What made you leave Houston?"

"Mostly, I was restless," I admitted. "That last year, I took a few trips with some buddies I worked with at the club. We went to New Orleans for Mardi Gras. Dallas and San Antonio for a weekend here and there just to break things up. After the last trip, I realized it was time for a change of scenery."

"What made you come back to California?"

"The ocean. The sunshine. The air. Those days I walked to San Diego were some of the best. I'd camp out where I could and wake up to the sound of breaking waves. Even when I got there, I didn't have money for an apartment right away, so I slept on the beaches and did my best to avoid cops. So I went back to San Diego for a couple of years. Decided I hated the city. Realized I didn't have time to surf when I worked eighty hours a week. That's when I went back to Temecula."

It was part of the truth. The other part was not something I felt like sharing.

"After I had my bearings as a realtor, I started looking for another town again." And because for the first time, there had been nothing tying me to Temecula.

"Still restless?" Clara smirked.

I chuckled. "Something like that."

"How'd you find Elyria?"

"From all that walking I did from LA to San Diego. Most of my trip was just about getting from one point to another, but the night I stayed here, I actually paid attention to the town. I slept on the same beach we went to today. Never forgot it. There was this restaurant close by that served the best chips and salsa I'd ever had. After Temecula, I decided to come and see if that restaurant was still in business. It was. So I moved here so I could eat there every day if I wanted."

"And you didn't take us there tonight for chips and salsa?" she asked, pretending to be offended.

"Tomorrow. We'll go there tomorrow." If all I had was two days with her, I was going to take them.

August slammed into the table, his hands cupped and

ready to receive some change. "Mom, can I have more quarters?"

Clara checked the time on her phone. "No, sorry, bud. I think we'd better get going."

"Not yet," he pleaded.

"Did you want to swim before bed?"

He thought it over, his mind visibly weighing the options. Then with a nod, he said, "Swimming."

I raised my hand for the waitress and the check. Then I left some cash on the table to pay our tab and escorted Clara and August to the Cadillac.

"Are you sure you want to go swimming?" I asked August. "Because I know this ice cream spot on the beach and—"

"Ice cream!" He jumped. "I want ice cream."

"Probably should have asked you first," I told Clara.

She waved it off. "I never say no to ice cream."

"Neither do I." I grinned as we all climbed into the car and set off down the road.

Even for a Sunday evening, the beach was full of people walking. The line at the ice cream hut was twenty deep. We debated the best flavor as we waited our turn to get waffle cones and set out for an evening stroll across the sand.

August ate his kid's cone faster than I'd ever seen a human consume ice cream before. Then he looked to his mother for permission to chase the seagulls.

"Not too far, okay?"

"Okay." He handed her a wadded-up, sticky napkin, then took off running.

"Maybe he'll burn off some sugar before bed." She frowned at the napkin, then shoved it into a pocket of her shorts.

August chased a bird, then spun around and raced toward us, only to turn around and find another distraction. But he stayed within shouting distance.

"It's your turn," I said as we settled into an easy pace. "How was Vegas?"

"Vegas was exciting. For a time. Aria hated it. She only lasted a month."

My footsteps stuttered. "You were there alone?"

I should have gone with her. *Son of a bitch.* I should have gone to Vegas. But never, in my wildest dreams, had I imagined Aria would leave her sister. And vice versa. Those two did everything together.

"Sort of." She shrugged. "But I was busy. I got my GED. A driver's license. We found an apartment in a not-so-great neighborhood, but the rent was cheap enough for me to afford on my own. I worked hard and things fell into place. Aria did the same, just in Oregon. We talked on the phone a few times a day. So not really alone, but on my own—if the difference makes sense."

"Yeah," I muttered. It made sense. But I still didn't like it.

She shouldn't have been alone. Clearly, she'd survived

and thrived but that was not what I'd wanted for her. Clara was tough, but she'd had it hard enough.

"How'd you come to work for Brody?" I asked.

"Aria went into hospitality. There were so many hotels with tons of jobs to choose from and the pay was better than anything we'd had before. I didn't want to clean rooms, so I waited tables to start with until I got my GED. Not long after, Brody's company, Carmichael Communications, hired me as a receptionist."

I could see her doing that, being the smile that greeted people when they walked through a door. A damn fine greeting.

"I didn't start working for Brody right away," she said. "I sat at the front desk for a while and as new positions opened up, I'd apply. Then when Brody's personal assistant quit, I put my name in for that too. I've been working for him ever since. When he decided to move from Vegas to Arizona, he asked me to come along. It was time for a change, so that's where we've been since."

"Ah." I nodded. "And that's how Aria met him?"

"Yes, but they hated each other." She laughed. "Last year, I was supposed to go to a wedding as Brody's plus-one, but I got this nasty cold, so Aria went in my place. It wasn't until then that they'd managed a civil conversation. Even afterward, things were dicey for a while. But the baby brought them together. Trace. They just named him the other day."

"Trace. Cool name."

August came racing in our direction with a shell in his hand. He held it up, just long enough to get a smile and a wave from Clara, then he tucked it into the pocket of his shorts and raced away.

"He turns six next month. I feel like I woke up one day and he was this little boy. My baby vanished before my eyes."

"And his father?"

Clara took a few steps, not answering. Her shoulders were stiff. Her smile gone.

"Forget it. I'm prying."

"No, it's just . . . it didn't work out. He's not involved in August's life and I prefer it that way."

What the hell? When? I opened my mouth to tell her never mind, I *was* going to pry, but she took off, jogging to catch up to August.

Well, shit.

For most people, I would have let it go. It wasn't any of my business. But this was Clara. Years apart, and she was still . . . mine. My business.

I hustled to catch up, and now that Clara was with August, her smile had returned, as gorgeous as ever.

She bent to inspect another shell, then when she spotted me, gestured to the parking lot. "Let's head back. Maybe you can still get some swimming in, bud."

"Yes." He fist pumped and ran in the direction of the car.

"I'm sorry," I said as we walked.

"It's fine." She waved it off. "It's in the past. As long as August is happy, I'm happy."

"He's a good kid. You're a good mom."

She looked up at me and smiled. "Thanks. That means a lot."

I nudged her elbow with mine. "It's good to see you."

"Same here." A lock of hair flew into her face.

Instead of tucking it behind an ear like I wanted to, I shoved my hands in my pockets. "I get you tomorrow, right?"

She nodded. "Our schedule is wide open."

"Good." The back of my hand brushed against hers, and for a second, I nearly took her hand.

She hadn't hugged me today. She used to hug. A jolt of electricity zinged to my elbow. Maybe it was the waves, but I swore I heard her breath hitch.

I inched away. I put space between us and did my best not to think of the last time I'd touched Clara.

It had been the night before we'd left the junkyard. She'd been in my arms after we'd had sex. There'd been no fumbling touches like our first time. There'd been no fear or worry. We'd come together like two people who'd been lovers for years, not a day.

A night I'd never forget.

"August!" she called, waving him back to us.

Yeah. Let's keep August here. Maybe with the kid close, these very intimate, very sexual, very naked thoughts about his mother would stop.

Christ, I was a fucking asshole.

"You should take the Cadillac," I said as we hit the lot. "Keep it while you're here."

"You don't mind?"

I shook my head. "Not at all. Still doesn't feel like my car."

"Okay. Thanks. That will make life a little easier for us to get around town tomorrow."

We all climbed in the car and I aimed us toward my house. "I've got some work to do tomorrow, but if you're up for it, I'd like to see you again for dinner. Chips and salsa?"

"We're up for it."

"And swimming in the ocean," August said.

Clara laughed. "You got it, bud."

The drive to my place was short, too short. The day had gone by too fast. I had this niggling fear that once Clara left California, I wouldn't see her again.

For years, I'd held on to hope that since she hadn't said the word *goodbye*, it hadn't been goodbye. Even after I'd looked her up and seen her with him. Foolish hope had stuck to me like grains of sand between my toes.

This time around, I doubted it would turn out the same. Though maybe it was for the best if I didn't see her again given the circumstances.

Why hadn't she come a year ago?

The sun was only beginning to go down as we parked in front of my garage. Orange tinged the horizon.

"Catch the sunset from your hotel if you can. They've been pretty lately."

Clara nodded and got out of the Cadillac, meeting me in front of the hood. "Thank you for dinner. And today."

"No thanks needed. It was, well . . . my head is still spinning. I look at you and can't believe you're here."

The color crept into her cheeks as another tendril of hair blew across her mouth. And damn it, my hands weren't in my pockets. They acted of their own accord, lifting to brush the blond strands away.

Clara's eyes were waiting as my hand fell away. And the look she gave me, the longing, twisted me into a knot.

"Clara, I—"

The door to the house opened and Holly emerged, walking down the sidewalk to the driveway. She was still in her baby blue scrubs from work and her dark hair was tied up. "Hey, baby. There you are. I texted you when I got here."

"Hey. Sorry. I haven't checked my phone."

"That's all right. Who's this?"

I couldn't look at Clara as Holly came to my side, standing on her toes to brush a kiss to my bearded jaw. "I want you to meet someone."

"Okay." Holly smiled at Clara, then glanced at the car. When she spotted August, she lifted her hand and waved.

I couldn't avoid Clara's gaze any longer. Anyone else would have just seen her smile. But I wasn't anyone. I'd learned to read her a long time ago and there was pain there. Hurt that was totally my fucking fault.

"Holly, this is Clara Saint-James." I swallowed hard, making the most painful introduction of my life. "Clara's an old friend. She lived with me at the junkyard."

Holly gasped, then lunged to take Clara's hand and shake it. "What? Oh my goodness. It's so nice to meet you."

"You too." Clara's smile widened. Too wide. She looked to me for an explanation.

I only had one to give.

"Clara, this is Holly Fallon. My girlfriend."

CHAPTER ELEVEN

KARSON

"And their tongues weigh as much as an elephant."

"That's a big tongue," I said.

August nodded, barely taking a breath between facts. "And you can tell how old they are from their ear wax."

"No kidding." I glanced at Clara, hoping to catch her gaze, but she was staring at her son. Just like she had been the entire meal. Eye contact had been fleeting at best.

"You sure know a lot about blue whales," Holly said, leaning into my side.

Gus beamed. "We learnded about them in school."

"Learned," Clara corrected.

"That's what I said."

She shook her head and smiled, then focused on the restaurant, taking in the colorful décor and other patrons. Again, looking everywhere but at me.

Holly and I were on one side of the booth, August and

Clara the opposite. Only a basket of chips and two bowls of salsa separated us, but for the tension between Clara and me, it might as well have been the Grand Canyon.

Thankfully, Holly hadn't seemed to notice. Neither had August. Clara had smiled politely as we'd gathered at the hostess station, just like last night when she'd shaken Holly's hand.

Maybe I was making too much out of this. Clara seemed . . . fine. She was laughing with her son and had gushed over her first chip and salsa bite. Was it just me?

She hadn't flirted with me yesterday. She hadn't acted strangely. Maybe it was my own bullshit making this weird.

How could it not be weird? I was attracted to Clara. I doubted there were many men on the planet who wouldn't find her alluring. Add that to the emotional connection I'd had with her years ago and I was as enchanted by her as I had been as a kid.

For that, the guilt was eating me alive.

I hadn't slept much last night. Holly had stayed over like she did most nights lately. Never in my life had I been so glad for a period week. I hadn't had to come up with a reason to skip sex. I just . . . it didn't feel right. I didn't feel right.

Holly and I had been dating for a year but she kept her own place. We'd talked about her moving in after her lease expired, but I hadn't insisted on it. She had a key. She knew she was welcome anytime.

The only night it had ever bothered me was last night. She'd curled into my side and I'd felt like a total fucking son of a bitch because while I'd been in bed with one woman, I hadn't been able to get my mind off another.

After tossing and turning for a few hours, I'd finally given up and disappeared into my office. Hours of sifting through paperwork and emails hadn't done anything but give me a headache.

I just . . . I needed a sign from Clara that we were good. That we were friends and whatever I'd been feeling yesterday was one-sided. *Look at me.*

She wiped a bit of salsa from the corner of August's mouth.

Look at me.

She plucked another chip from the basket.

Clara, look at me.

She brushed a crumb from her lap, then locked her attention on her son.

Goddamn it.

August was the true champ tonight. That kid had filled every second with all the facts stored in his little head.

"We learnded about skeletons too," he said.

"I like skeletons." Holly leaned forward. "I'm a nurse so I know lots about skeletons."

"Did you know the femur is the largest bone in your body?"

She nodded. "I did know that."

"The smallest bone is in your ear. It's the . . ." His forehead furrowed. "I can't remember the name."

"Stapes."

"Yeah, yeah." His eyes lit up. "The stapes."

"What was your favorite thing about kindergarten?" I asked.

"Recess."

I chuckled. "I liked recess too."

"Karson said you guys live in Arizona." Holly sipped from her margarita. "He actually told me about all of it. The Cadillac and how you came to bring it here. It's so fantastic. The whole trip across the country. Truly . . . wow."

"It's been incredible to connect with everyone again." Clara smiled and lifted her own drink, sparing me just a quick look over the rim. "I sent the girls a text last night. They all wanted me to tell you hello. And Londyn said she's sending you the title to the car before you try to do something stupid like return it."

I chuckled. "I'll have to get her number from you."

Somehow, I knew it wouldn't be strange talking to Londyn again. And somehow, I knew the feeling I'd had yesterday with Clara, that longing, wouldn't be there with my former girlfriend. Londyn and I would talk as old friends because that door had closed a long, long time ago.

No way could I say the same about Clara.

I took a chip, scooped some salsa and chomped it with fury. What the hell was wrong with me? Clara was an old friend too. We were history. So why couldn't I shake the feeling from yesterday? Why did it feel like I was on the wrong goddamn side of this booth?

Holly deserved better than this.

I just had to get through today and life would go back to normal. Clara was leaving tomorrow, and I'd put the memories in the past. Move forward.

"What did you guys do today?" I asked, eating another chip.

Clara glanced up, then her eyes skidded away.

Yeah, this hadn't been one-sided. I could fool myself all I wanted but she'd felt that spark yesterday too.

Fuck. I was such a prick.

"We spent most of the day at the beach," she said.

"I built a sandcastle," August said proudly, shifting to his knees so he could bend down and gulp his lemonade from the cup's straw.

"And we took one last drive in the Cadillac." Clara's eyes softened and she looked at me, really looked at me, for the first time this evening. "I hope you don't mind a few extra miles on her."

"Not at all."

"It's too bad you're leaving so soon," Holly said. "It would be fun to hear more stories about the junkyard. Karson rarely talks about it."

Because it wasn't a time I wanted to relive. I'd been angry and channeling a lot of false confidence. The stealing and the fights . . . I wasn't particularly proud of myself at that age.

"What's a junkyard?" August asked. The kid didn't miss much. Obviously, it wasn't something Clara had spoken to him about either. I doubted she would until he was older.

"It's a place where they take old cars and trucks that are broken," I answered.

"Do they get fixed?"

"No, not usually," Clara said. "They call it a junkyard because most of it becomes junk."

"Like garbage?"

She nodded. "Like garbage."

"What about the Cadillac then? It's not garbage."

"Sometimes, the best cars get rescued," I said. "That's what happened to the Cadillac."

"Oh. Sort of like my puppy stuffy that got ripped but Mom fixed it so we didn't have to throw it away."

I grinned. "Exactly."

August snatched a chip from the basket, content with the explanation. His curiosity was infectious, but the questions I wanted answers to weren't ones I could ask today. Mostly, I wanted to know about his father. Yesterday's attempt to broach the subject had backfired.

"Did you tell her about the junkyard?" Holly nudged my elbow.

"No. It, uh, didn't come up yesterday."

Holly thought the junkyard was an interesting piece

of my history. Like most people, unless they'd lived it, she didn't realize how hard it had been. How close I'd been to breaking so many times.

Maybe it was my fault for not explaining it to her. But why would I want to rehash the struggles? She'd gotten the glossed-over version of the past. To her, it had sounded like an adventure. Again, probably my fault for not painting it in a dirty, rust-tinged light.

That was part of why talking with Clara had been so easy yesterday. She understood. She'd always understood.

"What about the junkyard?" Clara asked.

Before I could answer, the waitress appeared with our meals. Even with the few minutes it took to get August settled with his quesadilla, when Clara looked at me for an answer, I still hadn't figured out exactly how to say it.

"The junkyard is . . . well, it's mine."

"Yours?"

I nodded. "Yeah. I own it."

"Did you buy it?" She set down her fork. "When you lived in Temecula?"

"No, I didn't buy it." I gave her a sad smile. "Lou left it to me. In his will."

"Oh." Her gaze dropped.

"Who's Lou?" August asked, his cheeks bulging with food.

"An old friend." Clara touched his hair, then focused on her plate. Though her fork only poked at her enchiladas.

"Are we gonna see him too?"

She shook her head. "No, bud. He . . . died."

"Oh." August looked down. "How?"

"In his sleep," I answered. "Surrounded by his collections."

The sadness in Clara's eyes broke my heart. "Did you see him often?"

"No. You know Lou."

"Yeah."

Lou didn't like visitors, even me. The few times I'd visited, I'd made sure to call ahead first. I'd gone in the morning. And only on the last visit had he actually invited me inside his shack.

The inside of Lou's home had looked much like the yard. There'd been piles stacked in hallways. There'd been shelves overloaded with books and boxes and binders. The kitchen counters had been so cluttered that the only free surfaces had been the sink and stove.

He'd led me through the maze and we'd sat at a small table, surrounded by his possessions. That was when he'd told me about Londyn and how she'd called for the Cadillac. How two days after that call, a fancy truck had shown up to haul it away.

I'd debated walking through the yard, but fear had stopped me, and instead, I'd left Lou to his solitude. I'd given him my card and told him to call me if he ever needed anything. That I'd stop by again.

He'd died before I'd had the chance.

Three months after the Cadillac had disappeared from the yard, so had Lou.

When his lawyer had called to break the news, and to inform me that Lou had bequeathed me all of his belongings, I'd nearly fallen out of my chair.

"I went to his funeral," I said. "I met his sister."

"He had a sister?" Clara asked.

"And two nieces. They were nice. Kind. They arranged for him to be buried beside his wife."

Clara's eyes bulged. "Lou had a wife?"

"She died young. In childbirth. Lou had been a mechanic back then. The junkyard had been in his family. After his wife and baby . . . he gave up his shop and moved to the shack."

"Lou." Clara pressed a hand to her heart.

"We didn't really know him, did we?"

"No, we didn't," she whispered, her eyes glassy.

August looked up at Clara with worry on his face. "Mom?"

"I'm okay." She shook away the sadness and smiled. "How's your quesadilla?"

"Good." He shrugged and took another large bite.

Holly leaned in closer, her hand finding my leg under the table. When I looked down, her brown eyes were waiting. They were the color of coffee, rich and warm. But they weren't as pretty as Clara's.

And I was a son of a bitch for making the comparison. *Fuck.*

"Maybe you should ask . . ." Holly nodded at Clara.

I gave her a slight headshake.

Either she missed it or ignored it, but when she turned to Clara and opened her mouth, it wasn't to eat. "Karson has been putting off going back to Temecula, but he finally is. On Wednesday."

"Seriously?" Clara's face whipped to me. "This Wednesday?"

"In two days." I lifted a shoulder. "Your timing is ironic. My plan was to go there tomorrow and check the place out before my meeting."

"What meeting?" she asked.

"There's a developer in Temecula who's trying to reclaim the area. He's building a housing development and wants to buy the junkyard. I agreed to meet him on Wednesday."

"Maybe you could go too," Holly suggested. "If you wanted to see it again and if you don't have to hurry home. I think it would be cool to go back to a place like that. See if it's changed. I work Wednesday through Sunday at the hospital, otherwise I'd go along. I've been wanting to see this junkyard since Karson told me about it."

Which was the reason I'd scheduled the meeting for a Wednesday. Holly was a supportive girlfriend, but this trip wasn't for her.

"Uh . . . no." Clara shook her head. "I don't think . . . no."

I nudged Holly, and this time, my headshake wasn't to be ignored.

She didn't know what she was suggesting. She didn't know the pain it could cause Clara to go back to that place.

Holly didn't even know the specifics of my childhood, let alone Clara's. All I'd told her about my past was that I'd had a bad relationship with my mother and run away at sixteen.

Dinner conversation was nonexistent after that. At least, between the adults. August came to the rescue once more, providing the entertainment with tales of kindergarten and a long list of his favorite toys. When the waitress came with the check, Clara insisted on paying the bill.

"You brought me a car," I said as we all walked outside. "You didn't need to buy dinner."

"I'm happy to. It was lovely to meet you, Holly."

"You too." Holly smiled. "I hope you keep in touch. Does Karson have your number?"

"I don't." I pulled my phone from my pocket, and when Clara recited hers, I sent her a text.

It dinged in her purse as she reached in to pull out the Cadillac's keys. Clara turned them over in her palm, holding them for one long moment, then she handed them over. "She's all yours."

"Thank you." The weight of the keys was too heavy. It wasn't just handing over a car, it was the end.

This was goodbye.

"I'll see you at home." Holly gave my arm a gentle squeeze. Then she gave August a fist bump and walked to my Audi, the two of us having driven it here to meet Clara tonight.

I'd drive her to the hotel. Then go home.

To Holly.

We loaded up and I pulled away from the restaurant, finding it hard to meet even the minimum speed limit. Cars began to pile up behind us but I couldn't press my foot into the gas pedal.

"Sorry. About Holly," I told Clara. "She doesn't understand."

"No apologies needed. Most people don't."

The air was warm as it rushed past our faces. August seemed so content in this car. One of his hands rested on the door as he took in the world around him.

The Cadillac made too short a trip and as I parked in front of the entrance to the hotel, my lungs wouldn't hold any air. The pain in my chest was crushing.

Clara was out the door the moment the tires stopped moving. She seemed in a rush to get August out of his seat and unclip the seat belt that had held it in place.

I got out, taking it from her to set it aside. "I could take you to the airport tomorrow."

"No, that's okay. We'll get an Uber."

"Mom, can we go swimming?"

"Sure, bud. Can you say goodbye to Karson?"

I knelt in front of him and held out my hand. "It was nice to meet you, August."

He grinned as he shook it.

"Ouch." I flexed my fingers after he let go. "Pretty strong kid you've got, Clara."

She put her hand around his shoulders, pulling him into her legs as I stood.

Then I memorized her face, one last time. The pink bow of her lips. The golden flecks in her eyes. The smile that woke me from my dreams. The breeze picked up her scent and carried it closer. Oranges and vanilla. Sweet. *Clara.*

"It was good to see you." My throat burned and the words came out in a rasp.

"You too."

I waited, wanting that hug. Clara had always hugged goodbye.

Instead, I got a wave and a small smile. "Take care of yourself, Karson."

"Yeah."

Then she was gone, ushering August inside with one hand while she carried his seat with the other.

She left me standing beside a Cadillac with a hole in my chest.

I stood there for a few minutes, staring through the glass doors to the lobby, hoping and wishing maybe she'd come back. But when the desk clerk gave me the fifth strange look, I unglued my feet.

This was the end.

"Goodbye, Clara."

The drive home was a blur, and when I walked through the door to find Holly in the living room with a book in her lap, for the first time, the sight didn't make me smile.

"Hey." She closed the book. "How'd it go?"

"Fine."

"Do you want to—"

"I'm going to go for a run." I walked away, but not fast enough to miss her startled expression.

I kept walking, disappearing to the bedroom to change. Then I was out the door, my feet pounding on the sidewalk to the beat of the music in my earbuds as I ran the couple blocks to the beach. When I hit the sand, I pushed harder. Faster. With every step, I willed Clara out of my mind.

There was a woman in my house who loved me. A woman who made me laugh. A woman who I cared for.

Holly didn't deserve this from me. I would do better.

Tomorrow, I vowed to do better.

Clara was returning to Arizona, and I would forget about her.

Or . . . try. I would try.

I pushed myself until my legs were burning and my lungs were on fire. Sweat dripped down my face and over my bare chest. I hadn't bothered with a shirt, I rarely did.

Three miles from home, I stopped and collapsed on

the sand, resting my forearms on my knees until I regained my breath. Then I sat there for hours, watching as the sunlight faded from the sky.

Tonight. I'd give myself tonight to mourn the loss of Clara again.

Then tomorrow I'd let her go. For good this time.

Lost in my own head, I jumped when my phone rang, the jogging earbuds I wore still locked in place. When I tugged the phone from my shorts pocket, I expected to see Holly's name on the screen.

But it was an out-of-state number. A number I'd memorized the same moment I'd typed it in earlier tonight.

"Hi," I answered.

"Hi," Clara said, her voice low. August must have fallen asleep. "Are you busy?"

"No." My heart raced faster now than when I'd been running.

"I was thinking about what Holly said. About Wednesday."

"Come with me." The plea in my voice was unmistakable. "I don't want to go alone. And I don't want to take Holly. She's the best. It's just that . . ."

"She doesn't get it."

I shook my head. "No one does."

"Okay," she whispered.

"Okay, you'll go?"

"I'll go."

I closed my eyes as a wave of relief crashed over my body. She was coming. Tonight hadn't been goodbye. "I'll pick you up around ten tomorrow."

The plan was to stay at a hotel tomorrow night before the meeting Wednesday. The drive back to Elyria wasn't long, but my meeting with the developer was at eight. With the regular morning traffic, it didn't seem worth the rushed commute.

"We'll be ready," she said.

I breathed. "Good night."

"Karson?" she whispered before I could hang up.

"Yeah?"

The other end of the line was silent other than her breathing.

"Clara?"

"Was it real?"

I closed my eyes. "It was real."

"It's been a long time, and I worried that maybe you were just a teenage boy and I was just a teenage girl and sex was . . . sex. Please don't take offense at that. We were young and I wouldn't blame you but—"

"It was real."

She went quiet again.

"You still there?"

"Yeah. Sweet dreams, Karson."

Then I'll dream of you. "Good night, Clara."

CHAPTER TWELVE

KARSON

"What made you change your mind?" I asked Clara. "About coming along."

"Aria." She glanced over from the passenger side as we rolled down the highway. "She asked me if I'd regret it in ten years. At first, I said no. But it nagged at me and I realized I need this closure."

"I can relate." I needed this closure too.

With Temecula. With the junkyard.

With Clara.

The top was up today to keep the wind and sun from August's face. And the exhaust. The trip from Elyria to Temecula was about an hour but if we hit traffic, it could take considerably longer.

So far, the road hadn't been too crowded, likely because it was midmorning on a weekday.

August was playing his Nintendo, something that

must be a treat because his eyes had gone wide when Clara had handed it to him. I suspected that Gus had been given a lot more video game time on this trip simply so the adults could talk without interruption.

"I think a part of me wants to go back just to remind myself of how far I've come," she said. "Or to remind myself that I won't ever have to go back."

"I felt the same when I moved to Temecula. It took me weeks to work up the nerve to drive to that side of town and when I did, it was at night. I parked outside the gate and just stared inside. Told myself I never had to survive those kinds of days again. So I get it."

She looked over again and smiled. "I know. Aria told me that if there was any time to go, it would be with you. She didn't want me going alone."

"Truth? That's why I've been avoiding this meeting. It was hard enough going back when Lou was there. Since he died, I only went once. And that was after his lawyer told me about his will. I drove up, left the car running, went to the gate and put a new padlock on the chain. Didn't even go in."

"So no one has been there in years?"

"No." I sighed. "I pay the electric bill every month. That's it."

"You said you went into his shack. Did you ever go look through the yard?"

I squirmed in my seat, not wanting to admit this was a

weakness. That a place full of rusted cars and metal parts had so far gotten the better of me. "Couldn't do it."

"Then we'll go together."

Was that why I'd never gone back? Because I'd been waiting for Clara to come with me?

She looked beautiful this morning. Her blond hair was pulled back into a braid that hung down her spine. The sheer cream blouse she wore was embroidered with lacey flowers. Beneath, a silky camisole clung to her frame. With a pair of jean shorts, she looked casual. Comfortable. *Sexy*.

I hated how the last word popped into my head with one glance at her toned legs. I hated how she'd walked out of the hotel lobby this morning and my heart had stopped. I hated that what I wanted most was to take her hand just to see if her fingers still fit between mine like they had when we were younger.

I hated myself for the thoughts running through my mind.

How fucked up was it that Holly had been the one to suggest this trip? While she was at work today, I'd been struggling to keep my mind off Clara.

Good thing was, the junkyard would be a distraction. Just setting foot in Temecula was sure to be strange for Clara again. Hell, it was still strange for me and I'd lived there as an adult.

Clara's phone rang in the purse at her feet. She bent to pluck the phone out and smiled at the screen. Then she held it up for me to see.

Londyn.

"Want to say hi?" she asked.

"Yeah."

Clara hit the screen, putting it on speaker, then held it up between us and let me answer.

"Hey, Lonny."

"Oh my God." She gasped at my voice. "Karson?"

My heart twisted. "It's me."

"It's you. I can't believe it." Her voice trembled. "Clara? Are you there too?"

"I'm here." She smiled, shifting sideways. "We're in the Cadillac. Karson is driving us to Temecula."

"Temecula? I thought you were going home today. I was calling to get the full scoop on Karson."

"Little change of vacation plans," Clara said. "First Temecula. Then we'll go home. Want me to call you later?"

"No way. I can't wait that long. It's been torture for the past two days. Tell me everything about Karson."

"Uh . . . I'm still here," I said.

"Good," Londyn said. "Fill in any blanks. And keep your eyes on the road. That car is nearly as precious as your passengers."

I chuckled. "I see you still love bossing me around."

"Hey, when you're good at something, why quit?"

Clara giggled. "Okay, what do you want to know about Karson?"

"Is he still handsome?"

"Yes." Clara's eyes darted to the seat, but I caught the flush rising in her cheeks. "He looks like Karson, just all grown up. He's got a short beard."

"A beard." Londyn groaned. "No. Not you too."

"What do you mean, not me too?" I asked.

"Brooks grew one and I hate it. Which I made the mistake of saying, so now he won't shave. He likes it because when he kisses Ellie it makes her giggle. But he has such a sexy jaw I hate that it's covered up with all that hair."

"In my defense, my beard usually only lasts a month, then I shave." I chuckled. Hearing her talk about her husband and daughter made my heart swell. "Are you happy, Lonny?"

"So, so happy." The smile in her voice filled the car. "Clara, what's his house like?"

"It's beautiful. It's white with warm touches. It's close to the beach. And clean, obviously. This is Karson we're talking about."

I barked a laugh. The girls always teased me for being the cleanest one in the junkyard. Not that they were messy, but I think they'd thought the token male would have left his things lying around. Except when you were living in dirt, the least you could do to take care of it was to put it away.

"Were you surprised? By the Cadillac?" Londyn asked.

"You could have knocked me over with a feather," I

answered. "What you did is nothing short of a miracle. But this car is too much."

"Shush. It was as much yours as it was mine."

"You put a lot of money into it. Let me pay for it."

"Never."

"Londyn—"

"Oh, look at the time. Gotta go. Drive safe. Clara, call me when you get home."

Clara giggled. "I will."

"It was good to hear your voice, Karson," Londyn said. "Expect a phone call from time to time."

"I look forward to it. And Lonny? Thanks. I'm not sure what I did to deserve this car I'm driving."

"You were the rock." Clara spoke for Londyn. "You were the glue. You saved us all when you found that junkyard."

"And that's why I want you to have that car," Londyn added. "Because if it makes you smile every time you get behind the wheel, then maybe you'll remember that you made me—us—smile through the hardest days. You deserve a lifetime of smiles. So take that car, drive it, and be happy."

My throat burned as Clara ended the call. She dabbed the corners of her eyes, then, as I'd expected, she twisted to look at her son.

August looked up and smiled before going right back to his game.

She drew strength from him. He rooted her. She anchored him. They relied on each other.

Once upon a time, she'd been a constant for me too.

My North Star.

"I'll have to get everyone's contact info from you," I said. "Now that I got to talk to Londyn, I'd like to say hi to Gemma, Kat and Aria too."

She nodded, her fingers flying over the phone's screen. "I'll text you their numbers."

Clara had been right about driving the Cadillac. It was a dream and every minute behind the wheel made me love it more. The hum of the engine and the gentle whisper of the wind took the place of any conversation as the miles disappeared beneath the tires.

Neither Clara nor I spoke of the question she'd asked me last night.

Was it real?

For twelve years she'd doubted the answer. Was it real?

Clara had been as real as the stars in the sky and the dirt below my feet. But at nineteen, I hadn't realized how much she'd meant. As a friend. As a lover. The sex had been incredible. Maybe I'd blown it up in my head because I *had* been nineteen and a guy and, well . . . it was sex. That had been fairly top of mind at that age.

When I'd walked away from the junkyard, I'd had no idea that Clara would stick with me. I guess I'd thought it would be like my breakup with Londyn. Just time to move on. But Clara had always been different, hadn't she? She'd always been there, like a quieter version of my conscience.

When I'd stop to catch a pretty sunset, I'd wonder if she was watching it too. When I'd sell a house, I'd hear her applause. When it was time to move on to a new town, I'd hope beyond all reason that I'd bump into her at the grocery store.

Now here she was.

If this was the universe's idea of ironic timing, it was a sick fucking joke.

Why now? When I'd finally decided to let go of the past. When I'd finally settled down in the town I planned to live in for the rest of my life. When I'd found Holly, the first long-term girlfriend I'd had in over a decade.

Time always seemed to be working against Clara and me.

As we reached the outskirts of Temecula, my hands tightened on the wheel. Tension crept up my spine, stiffening my shoulders and arms.

Clara fidgeted in her seat. Every minute she'd shift, tucking a hand under a leg or twisting to stare in a different direction.

Our exit approached and I dragged in a long breath, then hit the turn signal. *Here goes.*

"You okay?" I asked as I eased off the freeway.

"I don't know yet. Ask me later."

There was so much worry in her face, not even the large sunglasses could disguise it. Coming back here was always hard, especially after moving away. But my own anxieties vanished at the fear on her face.

I'd been here before. I'd lived here again. This trip was for Clara, and like Aria had said, she shouldn't do this alone.

"Where do you want to go first?" I asked. "Hotel? Or junkyard?"

"You said you wanted to check on the junkyard before your meeting tomorrow."

"Yeah, but we don't need to go there right away. We can get settled first at the hotel. Ease into this."

How people did this commute every day, driving in and out of California cities, was not for me. Most of the properties I sold in Elyria were for people who worked one, sometimes two hours away.

"I think . . ." Clara clasped her hands on her lap. "I think let's go to the junkyard before I chicken out."

"I'll be right here with you."

She looked over and some of the worry lessened. "I know."

I aimed the car in that direction. The hotel I'd booked was on the opposite end of town, next to the parks where they often launched hot air balloons. Maybe August would get to see one today or tomorrow.

Clara's nervous energy was palpable, growing with every block. Maybe August felt it too because he put his game down.

"Where are we going?" he asked, his eyes tracking my every turn of the wheel.

"To a place where Karson and I used to li—visit. A place we used to visit when we were younger."

"As kids?"

"No." She glanced behind us, giving him a soft smile. "Not as kids."

Adults would have called us kids. To August, a kid was probably someone his age. And the moment we'd run away, we'd stopped being kids.

"Is it a playground?"

"It's the junkyard."

"Oooh." He nodded. "With the broken stuff."

"With the broken stuff," she whispered.

Beyond the worry in her expression there was pain. Pain for the loss of her parents. Pain for the life she and Aria had lived.

Pain from being part of the broken.

The moment I pulled onto the road, Clara wrapped her arms around her middle, sitting stiff and rigid. Her eyes darted everywhere, taking it all in. "It looks different."

"The developer," I explained.

Gone were the other run down homes on this deserted road. No more fences to contain barking dogs. No more overgrown bushes. The street we'd traversed countless times was now a collection of barren lots. There was a spec home in the middle of construction, the crew pounding at nails on the roof. Side streets were being added to separate the land into square blocks.

A blank slate.

And at the end, the place we'd called home.

"I wondered if this road would ever change," Clara said. "There were days when I wished it would be swallowed in an earthquake. Others when I hoped it looked exactly the same just in case I ever needed it again."

I lifted a hand from the wheel, wanting to take hers, but I stopped myself and raked that hand through my hair instead.

Then, before either of us was ready, we were there.

The grasses around the junkyard's fence were as thick and unruly as ever. It looked unchanged from the day I'd left it behind. My heartbeat pounded in my ears as I slowed. Clara had her hand on the door, gripping it tight, like she wanted to keep it closed.

I did a quick U-turn so we could park on the same side of the street. Then I stopped us in front of the gate and put the Cadillac in park.

Clara stared out her window, seeing past the rusted chain and padlock to the mess beyond.

"We—"

She was out of the car before I could tell her we didn't have to go in.

I stayed in my seat and looked back at August.

His eyes were glued to the window. To his mother. "What's she doing?"

"Just looking."

Clara walked to the gate. She put her hands to the chain link, her fingers splaying between the holes. She stood there, her spine straight. Then she shoved away, and as quickly as she'd gotten out of the car, she was back in it, shaking her head. "This was a bad idea. I can't . . ."

"It's okay. Let's go to the hotel."

Her chin fell. "I'm sorry."

"Don't be. We'll come back tomorrow. And if you don't want to, that's fine too."

Clara nodded as her shoulders curled forward.

I put both hands on the wheel, holding it so I wouldn't hold her, and got us the fuck away from the junkyard.

"I'M SORRY ABOUT EARLIER." Clara pushed her sunglasses into her hair and turned to face me. "I didn't expect to feel so much. I thought once I saw it that I'd want to go inside."

"No need to apologize."

She gave me a sad smile. "I didn't expect it to hurt so much. Not having Lou there. Isn't that crazy? We didn't even know the man."

"Yeah, we did. We knew what mattered."

Lou had cared for us in the only way he'd been able. He'd given us a shelter. He'd given us protection. And he'd given us his secrecy. I couldn't have asked more from the man.

"Mom! Watch this one!" August jumped with all his might from the edge of the pool and did a spin before splashing into the water.

"We're in that stage. The *watch me* stage." Clara smiled and clapped for her son as he surfaced in the pool. "He'd live in the pool if he could."

"All right, I'm going in." An hour in the heat and I was ready for a swim.

I stood up from the lounge chair and stripped off my T-shirt. I tossed it away, glancing at Clara only to find her attention was on my torso. My chest. My arms. My abs. Unless I'd forgotten how to read attraction, there was lust in her eyes.

Christ. She wasn't making this easy on me.

Like she'd heard my thought, she ripped her eyes away, dropping her focus to her lap.

That was my cue to get the hell in the water. In three long strides I was at the pool's edge. I dove in, giving a long kick as I surfaced beside August.

He laughed, his arms spread wide with his water wings on his biceps helping to keep him afloat.

"Want to play a game?" I asked.

"Okay!"

Then I spent the next hour launching him into the air and crashing into the water. He laughed, we both did, every time.

Clara never moved from her chair. She stayed, watching. At first, she'd done it with a smile, but as the afternoon went on, the happy look on her face vanished. She almost looked . . . sad. Why would me playing with her kid make her look miserable?

Finally, after his fingers were pruney and the sunscreen Clara had smeared on him had most certainly worn off, she dragged her son to their hotel room to shower and get dressed for dinner.

They had a suite with a couple of bedrooms. My single was across the hall and we met in the lobby an hour later.

Much like last night at the restaurant in Elyria, August stole the show. He told me all of the things he wanted for his upcoming birthday and how he was having a pool party at Brody and Aria's house with six friends from his school. The kid was an exceptional buffer.

Every time I looked at Clara, every time my gaze lingered on the long line of her neck or the pretty shape of her ears, August would demand my attention.

Bless that kid.

And fuck my life.

When dinner ended and we walked back to the hotel, I was strung tight, ready to say good night and hit the pavement for another punishing run.

"Temecula is nice," Clara said as we reached the hotel lobby.

"Huh?" I'd been too busy staring at her ass in those

goddamn shorts because I was an asshole. A complete motherfucking asshole.

"The city. It's nice," she said as August pushed the button to call the elevator. "You get away from the shi— bad neighborhoods where we grew up and it's actually sort of charming with the Old Town wineries and hot air balloons."

We'd seen three balloons over the course of the day and each had enamored Gus.

"In another life, I would have stayed here," I said. "It is a nice town." But history tainted even the best of places.

"What made you leave? You said you always remembered Elyria. Was that why you moved?"

"No. I left because I didn't have to stay anymore."

"Have to?"

I gave her a sad smile as we stepped into the elevator. "For my mom."

"Oh."

"That's another discussion." I nodded at Gus. He didn't need to hear the gory details about the end of my mother's life.

The elevator carried us to the fourth floor and we all stopped in the hallway outside our rooms. Clara opened her door, letting August inside. "Thanks for dinner. And for your patience today."

"Do you want to go with me tomorrow? No judgment if you don't."

"Yeah." She seemed steadier now, like she'd conquered her fears. "I'd like to go tomorrow."

"Okay. Meet you in the lobby at about seven."

"Perfect. Good night, Karson." She turned to disappear into her room but the curiosity from earlier at the pool came rushing back and I shot out an arm, brushing my fingers along her elbow.

The shiver running down her body was visible.

The fire racing through mine was not.

"Why didn't it work out with August's dad?"

Clara's eyes closed. Her chin dropped. For the second time I'd pushed this subject. When was I going to learn to let it go?

"Sorry. I'll leave it alone. Good night, Clara." I dug the key from my pocket and unlocked my door. It was only after I'd taken one step inside that she whispered my name. When I turned, she had tears in those beautiful brown eyes.

"He wasn't you."

One sentence and she destroyed me. Then she rushed into her room, leaving me with the answer that I'd wanted to hear.

And the answer I had to forget.

CHAPTER THIRTEEN

KARSON

"I know I don't really understand what it was like for you back then, but I just wanted to tell you that I'm here if you need to talk," Holly said.

Because she was a good woman. And I didn't deserve her. "Thanks, babe."

"Call me later? After your meeting?"

"Yeah."

"Are you coming home tonight?"

I glanced over at Clara and August, standing beside the Cadillac. "I don't know. I was thinking I might stay another night, hang out, then take them to the airport."

"You should. Spend time with them. Relax. You've been working so hard. And we don't know when you'll see them again."

If only she knew what she was suggesting.

But I couldn't go home. Not yet. Not after Clara's

confession last night. Today was likely my last chance to get some answers, and I couldn't let her go, leaving me to wonder for the rest of my life.

"I'll let you know," I said.

"Okay. I love you." Holly had been saying *I love you* for months.

I hadn't said it back.

Maybe because I needed this closure with Clara. If I was going to move forward, I had to let this part of my life go.

"Have a good day at work. Bye."

"Bye." There was a hint of hurt in her voice. I suspected she'd cover it up with a smile, like she normally did whenever I didn't reciprocate those three words.

I raked a hand through my hair and over my bearded jaw, then shoved my phone away and walked to the car.

"Was that Holly?" Clara asked.

I nodded. "She just wanted to check in."

"She's very nice."

"Yes, she is."

I had a nice girlfriend. And because of it, my soul felt like it was being ripped in two. But now was not the time to deal with this. First, we had a job to do.

"All good?" I motioned toward the yard.

"I'm ready." Clara nodded and followed me to the gate.

The air was cool this morning as I unlocked the heavy chain. A breeze lifted the scent of rusted metal to my nose as I shoved the gate open wide enough to walk inside.

Clara followed close behind with August in tow. Her shoulders were pinned straight. There was determination in her gaze—yesterday's fears weren't going to stop her.

"This is a junkyard?" August shook his hand loose of hers and walked ahead of us both, turning in a circle to take it all in. Then he shrugged. "It's dirty."

I chuckled. Leave it to Gus to break the ice.

"Wow. Look at that." Clara walked past us, heading toward the side of Lou's shack. Her focus was on the green vines creeping along the exterior wall. "I didn't notice it yesterday."

The plant's roots stemmed from a black five-gallon bucket. A bucket I'd helped Aria fill with dirt years ago. Whatever vine she'd planted had not only survived under Lou's care, but it was growing wild. The far wall of his shack was nearly covered.

The plants had been here when I'd visited Lou, but over the past couple of years, they'd taken on a life of their own. With Clara running a fingertip over a leaf, it was beauty amidst the chaos.

"I'll be damned."

"Quarter." August marched up to me, hand out.

Digging a dollar bill from my pocket, I smacked it in his palm. Just yesterday he'd earned another one from me. I didn't realize how much I cussed until there was a kid to collect on every swear word.

"Aria is going to freak." Clara took her phone from her pocket and snapped a string of pictures. Then she held out a hand for August. "Your aunt Aria planted this a long, long time ago."

"She's a good planter."

"Yes, she absolutely is." Clara giggled, and with that musical sound, I was blasted twelve, nearly thirteen years into the past, when living in this junkyard had been hard. But damn, it had been good too.

Whatever tension I'd felt this morning after another sleepless night melted away. We could do this today because we were together.

I could do this today because Clara was here.

"Shall we?" I jerked my chin toward our end of the junkyard.

She nodded, giving August a smile, and then the three of us set off on a path that had once been as familiar as walking down the hallway in my own home. There was the large stack of old hoods that we passed first. Then a line of engine blocks that Lou had arranged by size. Then two stacks of tires, three rusted trucks to round and then...

"It's still there," Clara whispered.

The tent that Gemma had built was nearly unchanged.

The canvas tarp that had acted like the front door was pooled on the dirt, dusty and matted from years of enduring the elements. But the walls were intact. The sheets of metal and the tarp roof were still pitched together and solid.

"Wow." Clara surprised me, taking the lead and rushing for the doorway.

"What's in there?" August asked, dashing around her.

His curiosity lightened the mood. He saw it like a child, as a fort and an adventure. He saw it for what we'd once seen it for too.

Clara was close behind him as he ducked his head through the door. She nudged his shoulder and the two of them bent to step inside. I crouched and joined them, dropping to a knee to take a look around.

The air was stale and smelled of earth. The common room was the same. The paintings that Katherine had done in her bedroom were there, nearly as perfect as they had been because the walls had protected them from rain.

Clara took a picture of them too. "I don't know if she'll want to see them, but just in case."

She didn't take a photo of Gemma's room—the space that I'd taken after the girls had set out for Montana. The room where Clara had been mine. She wouldn't even look there. She wouldn't look at me either.

Was she thinking about those precious nights? Was she remembering? They were as fresh in my mind as yesterday. The softness of her lips. The sweet scent of her hair. The delicate touch of her hands.

No. Stop, damn it. Stop remembering. I shot to my feet

and went outside, shaking the past away. These fucking memories were killing me.

So were the words she'd said to me last night in the hallway.

We hadn't talked about it this morning. We'd spoken politely over breakfast, both of us counting on August to carry the conversation. Then we'd driven here in silence, and I'd stepped away to take a call from Holly.

"Now where?" August asked, bursting out of the tent.

Clara didn't answer her son. She just took off on the narrow path to where the Cadillac had once rested.

The hole where it had been was noticeable. Other parts and pieces had been pushed aside, probably to make room for the crew to haul it out of here.

I studied Clara's expression as she stared at the space. I'd give anything to know what she was thinking. To know if she was picturing two teenage kids staring up at the stars.

She gave me no insight before continuing down the path, her graceful steps a sharp contrast to the wreckage around us. Clara had always been too good for this place, but today, she especially stood out. Maybe it was the white dress she'd worn. Or the colorful flowers embroidered on the front that trailed from the neck to the hem that hit midthigh.

Did she always wear white? Since she'd come here, I'd only seen her in light colors.

I lingered behind her and August as they made their

way down the path. I knew exactly where she was headed, and I didn't want her to feel rushed because I was crowding her.

Funny how I'd needed her to come inside this place. But now that she was here, she didn't really need me. Not when she had August.

I'd never seen a mother-son duo like theirs. Maybe it was because she was his only parent—I assumed she was his only parent—but they had this bond. It was like a string tied between them, visible if you looked hard enough.

When I caught up to them, Clara was standing at the back of the delivery van, staring at the closed door.

August had left her side and was bent over the rusted can that Aria had once used to water her plants.

"Want me to open it?" I asked.

She sucked in a deep breath, nodding as she blew it out. "Yes."

The latch was rusted and stiff but after a hard tug, it sprang free. The scrape of metal on metal echoed across the yard along with an ear-splitting squeak as I lifted the door.

I hopped up into the back, surveying the space. Then I held out a hand to help Clara up so she wouldn't get that dress dirty.

She didn't let my hand go as she looked around. Her grip tightened when she saw the wreckage of old books and blankets shoved against the far wall.

An animal had gotten in here at one point and had turned the pages and cloths into shreds. A bed of its own.

Clara bent down, picking up something from the floor. The dry-erase marker. The one they'd used to track their countdown on the wall. She held it up, inspecting it for a moment, then tossed it into the mess. "It's small."

"It all feels small."

A place that had once felt so vast, like a continent of its own, had been reduced to its three acres by time and age and reality.

"I'm not taking a picture of this." She spun away, ripped her hand free and was on the ground before I could blink.

I took one last glance, wishing it hadn't been like this for Clara's sake, and left it behind, not bothering to close the door. Then I jogged to catch them on their way to the shop since I had the keys.

Going in first, I flipped on the lights. "I'm surprised so many work."

The smell of gasoline and oil was thick from years of sitting. I had no idea if the equipment would work, but I'd let someone else deal with that.

I checked my watch. It was nearly eight. "I'd better head out front to meet the developer."

"We'll come with you." Clara backed away from the shop and we all walked toward Lou's front door. "Did you decide what you want to do with it?"

"Sell it." Now that I'd come here and seen it again,

there was no reason to hold on to an old junkyard. "I'd like to go through Lou's shack. Make sure there isn't anything inside to keep. But there's nothing for me here."

"Not quite." Clara looked up at me with a sad smile. "There was something here. I think that's why Lou left it to you. Because he knew that you needed to come here and be the one to put it to rest."

I almost tripped over my own damn feet. "How do you do that?"

"Do what?"

"Say what I'm feeling but haven't figured out how to articulate."

Her eyes softened. "I'm glad we came here."

"Me too."

We rounded the corner just as a large white truck pulled up behind the Cadillac. A man in a nice pair of jeans and a button-down shirt hopped out, raising one hand to wave while he held a notebook in the other.

"Would you mind if I went into Lou's?" Clara asked.

"Not at all." I handed her the keys, then winked at August before going to shake the developer's hand.

I spent the next thirty minutes taking him on a tour of the junkyard. He told me about his plans for the neighborhood and the park he'd be adding on this section of land. Maybe it wouldn't happen, but I liked the idea of this being a place for kids to play. A safe place for future generations, like it had been for me.

"There's a lot here," I told him as we walked back to

his truck. "I don't have the time or energy to sift through it all. So I'll sell it to you, as-is."

"How much?"

"Make me a fair offer based on the valuation of the land."

He nodded. "I'll have my realtor draw it up today."

"Great." I shook his hand once more, waited until he was gone, then headed for the shack.

August was sitting at the same table where I'd once sat with Lou. He looked bored out of his mind with one hand holding up his head. When he spotted me, he sat up straight. "Can we go now?"

"Soon," I promised. "Where's your mom?"

"Back here," Clara called.

I found her in what had been Lou's office. Or library. Or notebook-hoarding room. "Um . . . whoa."

There were spiral-bound notebooks stacked against the walls in towering columns. Some almost as tall as me. Three bookshelves against the wall were so overloaded with books and binders that the shelves sagged in the middle beneath the weight.

"What's in these?" I slid a notebook off the top of a stack and opened it to the first page. It was a series of numbers on the left side with a sketch of a car's grill that took up the center. It had the make, model and year of the car it would have belonged to. At the bottom was a location. *Zone 4.*

"I think he had this entire place cataloged." Clara had

a few notebooks open on Lou's desk, flipping through them. Page after page was more of the same. "I bet he knew what and where every single piece was. These were his treasures."

I shook my head, unable to believe all that I was seeing. Lou must have spent years in here, detailing every scrap and every part on this property. I put the notebook back on the stack, then left the office, wandering deeper into the shack. Lou's bedroom was at the rear of the building, and unlike the rest of his home, it was clutter-free.

Everything was filmed with dust, but the emptiness of the room was utterly shocking.

A bed rested in the center of the space, pushed against the far wall. On either side were two nightstands. One held a box. The other a framed photograph. The picture drew me in, and I skirted the bed to get a closer look.

It was of Lou, barely recognizable as a younger man, seated with a woman wearing a yellow polka-dot dress. *His wife.* He had a smile on his face. He looked happy. He'd been a different man.

In a different life.

"When he lost her, he lost his way." Clara had snuck up on me and was peeking past my shoulder. With a sad smile, she went to the other nightstand, running her fingertips over the dusty box. Then she flipped the clasp to lift the lid and gasped at whatever was inside. "Karson."

"What?" I rounded the bed to her side, the photograph

of Lou and his wife still in my grip. There wasn't much to save here but this picture was definitely coming home.

"It's a letter. To you." She lifted it out, then narrowed her gaze at whatever else was in the box. "Wait. There are more."

She pulled out a stack of letters, sifting through them. Each had one of our names on top. Six letters for the six kids who'd lived here. There was more in the box, but my focus was on Lou's neat and tidy script and the envelopes in Clara's hands.

"Oh my God." She rifled through the stack again.

"I can't believe it."

She nodded. "He even spelled Londyn's name right. With a *y*. I didn't know he actually knew our names."

I blinked, unable to process what I was seeing.

"He left them for you to find," she said. "He put all of his stuff in the other rooms, but this one was clean because he wanted you to see this box and that photo."

Lou. I wished I'd known him better. I wished I'd come back again before he'd passed. "He noticed more than he let on, didn't he?"

"I think he noticed everything."

I tore my eyes away from the letters and met Clara's gaze. We were close. Too close. My chest brushed against her arm. Her hair, left long, draped between us and the ends tickled my forearms.

God, she was beautiful. Her tender heart. Her unwavering strength. I soaked her in, giving myself a moment to swim in those chocolate eyes.

My hand lifted, my fingertips desperate to trace the soft line of her jaw, when little feet pounded at our backs.

"Mom!"

She jerked, dropping her gaze. Then she inched away, as far as she could toward the nightstand, and cleared her throat. "In here."

"Can we go now?" August begged.

"Yeah." I took a step away from his mother. "We'd better go."

They'd better go.

For the first time since Clara had surprised me with the Cadillac, I was ready to send her back to Arizona.

Maybe if she was five hundred miles away, I'd actually be able to resist her.

CHAPTER FOURTEEN

KARSON

"How do you feel?" Clara asked as we drove away from the junkyard.

"Lighter. You?"

"Free."

Free. Not quite. But almost.

I wouldn't be free until I could let Clara go.

But for the moment, I was content.

We'd put the top down to get some fresh air. I drew in a long breath, holding it in my lungs. In the back of my mind, I heard the click of a door. The turn of a page.

A chapter had ended, and it was time to move on.

August was in his seat, playing with some metal rings he'd found at Lou's and had asked to keep. Beside him was the box that contained Lou's letters and whatever items he'd stored beneath.

Clara and I hadn't spent time looking through them.

Gus had been antsy to get out of there and since he'd been such a trooper all morning, we'd locked everything up and left.

"Think you'll come back here in twenty years?" Clara asked as we rolled down the road and put the junkyard in the rearview. "See what it's like?"

"Maybe. You?"

She shook her head. "Probably not. I'm glad I got to see it again. I feel like that door is closed now."

"I was just thinking the same damn thing."

"It's a good reminder of how far we've come and why I'm working so hard to make sure August never has that sort of life."

"You're a good mom, Clara."

"That's the best compliment you've ever given me."

"Ever? What about the time I told you that you were the prettiest girl in the universe?"

"That was because you were a shameless flirt."

"With you?"

"Always," we said in unison.

Clara closed her eyes, scrunching up her nose.

I cringed.

Back to awkward then. Because I couldn't seem to help myself.

Why couldn't I just see her as my friend? Completely platonic. Why? The answer was buried deep and at the moment, I was not going to acknowledge it. I *couldn't* acknowledge it.

The trip to the junkyard had been another distraction to shove it all away, but now that the meeting was over, the nagging guilt came rushing back.

"Sorry." I ran a palm over my chin.

Maybe it was time to shave. Holly would hate it. She loved the beard. Did Clara? *It doesn't matter, asshole. She's not your girlfriend.*

"I'd better get some gas," I said, needing a task and a moment to pull my shit together. We were in the middle of town and I stopped at the next station. When I pulled in beside the pump, I got out and stayed out, hovering beside the tank, letting the guzzling sound from the nozzle block out Clara's muted conversation with Gus.

One more night.

I'd swim with August this afternoon. We'd have a nice dinner. Then tomorrow I'd take Clara to the airport and put this behind me. For good.

Holly deserved better.

And fuck, so did Clara. She needed to find a man who was free.

The tank was nearly full when a door opened and Clara stepped out of the Cadillac, her wallet in hand. "August earned a treat for being so good this morning. Want anything?"

"Nah. Thanks."

She gave me a small smile and turned, but instead of walking across the lot, she froze. Her entire body turned to stone.

"Clara."

She didn't answer. Instead, she stared forward at the convenience store where an older man had just come out the door with a plastic sack in his hand.

Abandoning the gas pump, I rounded the trunk and went to her side. "Hey. What's wrong?"

She gulped and nodded at the man. "That's him."

The man had thinning brown hair and a splotchy pallor to his face. He pulled a cigarette from his pocket and placed it between his lips. His frame was thin beneath his shirt, the bones of his shoulders trying to cut through the cotton.

When he glanced our way and those beady eyes narrowed on Clara, her body flinched.

"Your uncle," I guessed.

I hadn't seen the guy before, not that I'd needed to. There wasn't a person on earth who was likely to get this reaction from Clara. And Gemma had seen him once, ages ago, and the way she'd described him fit this man perfectly. A total fucking creep. That hadn't changed.

And the rage I'd felt toward that man hadn't dulled either.

My fists balled at my sides. When Clara had told me about her uncle, I'd wanted to kill the bastard. The anger was still there, an inferno churning in my veins. Hungry for a victim.

I took a step forward, ready to walk over and make that son of a bitch pay for all that he'd done to them, but before

I could take my second step, Clara's hand slipped into mine.

She clutched it, not holding me back, just holding on.

Her gaze was still glued to him as he stared back. She kept her shoulders straight, her chin held high. She didn't cower. And the glare she sent him was nothing short of murderous.

A swell of pride mixed with my rage. Good for her. Damn, but she was strong.

It took a moment, but he recognized her. His bony frame tensed. He gave her a sideways look, and then he was gone, scurrying to his nineties-model Honda Civic, the tires squealing as he raced out of the station's lot.

And Clara just held on, staring at the spot where he'd been.

"He tried but he didn't ruin us," she whispered.

"No, he didn't."

"He knew who I was."

"Yes, he did."

"We were scared of him as kids. We knew it was wrong but not how to fix it. We should have turned him in."

"You still can. You have the power here, Clara."

Her head tilted to the side. "You're right. We should have. I didn't get that as a kid but we're not those scared girls anymore. And we've been ignoring it, burying it. He deserves to pay. To be registered as a sex offender at least.

When we get home, I'll talk to Aria. We'll do what we can and then never think of him again."

"Good for you."

"Thank you," she whispered. Then she closed her eyes and finally, her shoulders sagged. "I really hoped that he was dead."

"Me too." Without hesitating, I spun her toward me and hauled her into a hug, wrapping her in my arms and feeling her cheek press against my heart.

Clara snaked her hands around me, and as tightly as I held her, she clung to me.

"I'm sorry," I said into her hair.

"They should have made a better plan. My parents. They let us down."

I stayed quiet. My hatred was aimed at her uncle, but there was resentment for her parents too. Resentment I hadn't understood as a teenager. Her mom and dad had let their daughters down by not having a better plan in case of their deaths.

Clara and Aria never should have been given to their uncle.

"What can I do?" I asked.

"You're doing it." She relaxed, giving me her weight.

The scent of orange and vanilla filled my nose as I rested my chin on her head. Having her in my embrace felt so familiar. So . . . right.

I should let her go. *Let her go.*

I didn't move.

"Do you still hug everyone goodbye?" I asked.

"Yes."

"Then why not me?" I remembered that so clearly from our time at the junkyard. Whether it had been in town when she'd go one way and I'd go the other, or even when she caught me at the junkyard before I'd leave for the day. Every goodbye had come with a hug. Most hellos too.

Until now. Last night, there'd been no hug.

Not once since she'd come to Elyria had she touched me.

Clara loosened her grip on me and slid her arms free. Then, too soon, she was gone and there was a gulf between us.

I'd asked the question.

But she didn't answer.

We both knew the answer would only make this worse.

"I'd better get August his treat." She pointed to the store, but the crease between her eyebrows told me she didn't want to go inside.

"What does he want? I'll grab it."

She opened her wallet, but I waved it off. "I've got it. I'm going to get some water too."

"Skittles or Swedish Fish or Starbursts or Twizzlers. He loves fruity candy."

"Got it." Then I got the hell away.

Fuck. Maybe we should say our goodbyes tonight and

I should go home. That would be the smart thing to do. Call it over and done with.

Instead, I bought August's candy and listened to him tell me about which color combinations of Skittles were the best as we drove to the hotel. Then we went swimming for a few hours while Clara looked on from a lounge chair.

Entertainment at dinner was once again provided by the five-year-old, and when we returned to the hotel, I had this sinking feeling that I wasn't going to see him again. In just a few days, August had made a lasting impression.

I'd miss dinners without a nonstop stream of interesting facts that he learned at school. I'd miss the excitement that seemed to pour from every word.

But if I couldn't control these feelings about Clara, then I had to cut off contact. I'd done it for twelve years, so what was a lifetime more?

No Clara meant no Gus. I'd miss out on seeing him as a teenager. A young man. An adult. There was a twinge in my chest as he pushed the elevator button. I couldn't tear my eyes away from his smile and his small hands and the slight waves in his dark-blond hair.

Was this why Clara was always looking to him? Because she knew how fast he would change?

My throat was dry as we stepped into the elevator and rode to our floor. As Gus raced down the hallway toward the room, my steps dragged like I was wearing lead-filled shoes.

Clara's steps seemed even shorter and heavier than mine.

This was goodbye. There was the trip to the airport in the morning, but that would be full of logistics, baggage and a rushed farewell.

"Can we rent a movie?" August asked, standing beside their door.

"Sure." Clara nodded.

"Want to watch with us?" he asked me.

I opened my mouth to let him down gently, but then Clara answered for me. "Yeah. Watch with us."

"Okay." Reckless, but that was my defining trait this week.

So we went inside her room, the three of us settling on the couch in the common room in her suite, with August in the middle, and rented a movie.

Gus fell asleep halfway through the musical cartoon.

"This is more excitement than he's used to," Clara said, turning down the volume on the TV.

"He's such a great kid. Maybe the best I've ever met."

She smiled down at him as he slumped into her side. "He's pretty fantastic, isn't he?"

"I have to tell you something," I said. "Probably should have admitted it sooner."

"What?"

"I looked you up on Facebook."

Her eyes widened. "You did? When?"

"About six years ago. I was curious. Temptation got

the better of me and I wanted to know that you were okay. You didn't have much posted but a few pictures. I saw one of you and him together. You looked happy. In love. It was hard to see."

So I hadn't looked her up again. Clara or Londyn or Gemma or Katherine. I'd taken it as a sign to move forward. Easier said than done.

"I assume the guy was Gus's father. What happened?"

She sighed. "About what I said last night. I'm sorry. I shouldn't have. I know it put you in an uncomfortable position with Holly and . . . I'm sorry."

"It's okay." If only she knew the real reason that I was uncomfortable had nothing to do with her words, but the words I wanted to say back.

"I met Devan in Las Vegas." She stared at the TV as she spoke. "I'd been living there for years and work was mostly my life. It was rare that I did anything exciting, but one weekend some friends dragged me to a nightclub. That's where I met him."

Green crept under my skin but I stayed expressionless, listening. "How long were you together?"

"About a year. I should have ended it long before that. But Devan had his moments when he was wonderful and funny and loving. Whatever pictures you saw were probably from those times. But the longer we were together, the more I realized that those good moments were only because he knew I was about to call it off. Then he'd charm me, and I'd fall for it. I'd forget that he was a narcissist, and I was only a beautiful decoration in a world that revolved around him."

How could anyone in Clara's presence not want to fall into *her* orbit? This guy Devan must have been blind.

"I got pregnant. Obviously. It hadn't been planned, but he accused me of doing it on purpose even though I'd been on birth control."

"Seriously?"

She shrugged. "A baby meant Devan wouldn't be the center of attention. To this day, I don't know if he ever believed that it was an accident. We'd fight about it. I'd tell him we were done. He'd apologize and we'd be good for a week. Until we weren't. It was this sick, unhealthy cycle, but I didn't want to let him go. Not for me, but for August. I was sure that if I could just get Devan through the pregnancy, he'd meet our son and realize that love wasn't a competition. That there was enough for him and a baby."

"Did he?"

"No." She tore her eyes away from the wall, dropping them to August. "By my third trimester, he was already checked out. I suspected he'd already found another woman who'd worship him. I was an afterthought by then. When August was a newborn, I told him we were done. He didn't argue."

"Has he been involved at all?"

"No. Devan was never going to change. He was never going to make a good father. I didn't want to put August through any disappointment when Devan made a promise he couldn't keep. So I gave him an out. I wouldn't ask for any money or support if he signed over all of his parental rights. Ask me if he put up a fight."

Of course he hadn't, the dumb son of a bitch. "I'm sorry you went through all that alone."

"Don't be. I had Aria. And Brody. Not long after that, Brody told me he was moving to Welcome, Arizona, and asked if I wanted to come along. A new town. A fresh start. It was a no-brainer."

Had Brody always planned on offering Clara the opportunity in Arizona? Or had he offered after the fallout with Devan? I had a feeling I wasn't the only man who did what he could to protect her.

Regardless, Clara and Aria were good allies to have in your corner. Brody was a lucky man to have them both.

Clara blew out a long breath. "After I broke it off with Devan, I'd go through these days when I was so mad at myself for not seeing through his façade. He was . . . attractive. I'm not proud to say that I let his looks cloud my judgment. But when August was a baby, one day I just stopped being mad. At myself. At Devan. I got the best part of him and he was too self-absorbed to realize that when I left Vegas, I took that piece with me."

"I like the name August."

She gave me a sad smile. "That was my dad's name. Did I ever tell you that?"

"No."

"If I'd had a girl, I would have named her after Mom.

Hopefully Aria will have another baby one day and if it's a girl, she can take that name. Millie. That was her name."

"Pretty name."

"I like it too." She shifted, turning slightly sideways on the couch so August's head rested in her lap.

The muted light from the TV cast a light glow over the room. They caught the gold flecks in her gaze, making them dance.

How could he have let her go?

How could *I* have let her go?

Two stupid men.

"I should have come to you anyway. Despite the Facebook pictures. I assumed you were happy and had moved on, but I should have come to find you."

"Except then I wouldn't have August." She gave me a sad smile. "Timing was never on our side, was it?"

"No, it wasn't." If I had looked her up a year later, after Devan had been out of the picture, or if she had come here a year earlier, before Holly . . .

Or if at nineteen, I hadn't been so wrapped up in my mother's words.

You're a piece of shit, Karson. You're worthless.

Get out of my sight. I hate you. I hate looking at you.

You are nothing. A disgrace. You're a fuckup.

"My mom died," I blurted.

Clara tensed. "When?"

"Not long before I moved to Elyria. After she died, I wanted to get out of Temecula for good."

"Is that why you came back here? When Gemma hired the PI the first time, he'd said you were here. That always seemed so crazy to me. I figured you'd be long gone like the rest of us."

"Yeah." I sighed. "I got a call one day when I was living in San Diego the second time from a police officer here in Temecula. Mom had been in a car accident and was in a coma."

"Karson, I'm so sorry."

"Should I tell you this? It might be hard to hear."

"Drunk driver?" she guessed. Her own parents had been killed by a drunk driver, and the last thing I wanted was to cause her any pain.

"Yeah." I nodded. "I'd expected the drunk to be her, but it wasn't. I think that's the only reason I came back. If she had hurt someone . . . well, there's a lot I struggle to forgive my mother for. That would have been a deal breaker."

"You came back to take care of her, didn't you?"

"She probably didn't deserve it. But I did it anyway." I lifted a shoulder. "It took me a long time to learn that she was sick. That she hated herself so much that it was all she knew. That her taking that hate out on me was because I was the only person she had. And it took me a long time to let go of her ghost. To realize I was not the person she told me I was."

"You're a good man, Karson Avery."

I dropped my eyes to August, curled up between us.

This kid didn't even know how lucky he was to have a mother like Clara.

"After she passed, I felt like I could leave it all behind. That's when I moved to Elyria."

"Your fresh start."

I nodded. "We all needed them, didn't we?"

"We did." Clara gave me a sad smile. August squirmed on the couch, an arm flailing in the other direction. Clara scooped him into her arms and pushed up off the couch, carrying him to the adjoining room. The rustle of clothes and the thud of shoes dropping to the floor was my hint to leave.

It was time. It was time to say goodbye. To get back to life in Elyria.

To Holly.

She and I had a shot. We had a chance at a future. I hadn't felt like that about any woman I'd dated before, not Londyn. Not even Clara. Not the women I'd met along my way. Mostly because I'd been too young, but with Holly, there was a real chance.

Like Clara said herself, timing had never been on our side. Maybe that was for a reason.

I waited for Clara to finish with August. She emerged, closing his bedroom door. Then I spoke the words I'd been dreading all evening. "It's been so great to see you. To meet August."

"You too."

"Good night, Clara." I spun for the door, ready to make my escape, when she stopped me.

"Wait. What about the box?" Clara went to the small table where we'd left Lou's box and letters.

The box. Damn it.

"Oh, I forgot about it." In an effort to get out of here while I still could, before I said or did something that would tarnish these days with Clara, I'd completely forgotten about the box.

The door would have to wait.

She took a chair on one side of the table while I sat in the other. Then she lifted out the box's contents. Other boxes, all small. "These are jewelry boxes."

Six in total, in varying colors and sizes. And each of them had a small piece of paper taped to the underside.

"Here you go," she said, passing over my letter and the navy velvet ring box with my name on it.

I opened the envelope first, pulling out a crisp piece of ecru paper and unfolding it.

KARSON,

These were my wife's rings. She couldn't wear them when she was pregnant with our baby because her fingers swelled up like sausages. That's what she called them. Sausage fingers.

By rights, I should have buried her with them. But that was a hard time. I'm ashamed to admit that I didn't realize she hadn't been wearing the rings in her coffin until I found them in her jewelry box a few weeks later.

Now that she's gone and I'm not long to follow, I'd like you to have them.

Give them to a woman like my Hope. She was smart and brave. She laughed through the good times and made me laugh through the bad. She was the soul on earth I was made to find.

I left a picture of her beside my bed. Wasn't she a beauty? One look at her and the world made sense.

Take care of yourself. And I'll thank you in advance for taking care of these for Hope. I trust you'll give them to someone special. You always had good taste in girls. I suspect that won't change.

Lou

I READ IT TWICE. Three times. And my heart ached so badly I could barely breathe.

It was an elegant letter for a man who'd mostly spoken in grunts. Refolding the paper, I returned it to the envelope, tucking it carefully inside. Then I took the box and pried the lid open.

The center jewel on the engagement ring was a deep grayish blue, the color of the ocean on a stormy day. It was accented by tiny diamonds on each side. The white jewels were arranged without a pattern, like leaves beneath a flower. The white gold band was smooth and shiny. It matched the simple wedding ring beneath.

"Damn, Lou." I pulled the ring from the box, holding it up to catch the light. "This was his wife's ring."

Clara didn't respond. She was too busy staring at the ring pinched between her own fingers.

It was Lou's wedding band. I didn't have to ask to know. And I suspected Clara's letter was also about Hope.

A tear dripped down her cheek, snapping her out of her trance. She blinked her eyes clear and swiped at her face. Then she refolded her letter and put it away. "I'll send the others their letters and boxes when I get home."

"Thanks." I put Hope's ring away, then shoved the box into my pocket. Then I took the letter and stood, needing a minute to let Lou's words sink in.

The timing of this had me reeling. Two months ago, that letter would have meant something else entirely.

"I'm going to go," I said. "Good night."

"Good night," she whispered.

I was almost to the door when she stopped me again.

"Does Holly know about us? About what happened in the past?"

My shoulders fell and I turned. "No."

She got up from the table and walked closer. "Aria never knew about us either. I always wondered if she did, but she never said anything."

"You didn't tell her? Why?"

"Because you were mine. You were the one thing I

didn't want to share. With anyone." Her confession rocked me to my heels. "Why didn't you tell Holly?"

"Because I fucked up," I admitted, the weight of Lou's letter settling on my shoulders.

"What do you mean?"

"I should have gone with you to Las Vegas."

A fresh sheen of tears flooded her eyes. "Sweet dreams, Karson."

"Then I'll dream of you."

I shouldn't have said it, but the words were unstoppable.

When I left, she let me go.

When the door closed, there was no turning back.

I drove the Cadillac home.

CHAPTER FIFTEEN

KARSON

"It's Clara, isn't it?" There were tears in Holly's eyes. "When you wake up in the middle of the night, it's because of her."

"Yes, it is."

Years of sleepless nights and it was almost always because of Clara. I'd dream that she was hurt. I'd dream that she was calling my name, begging for help. I'd dream that she was drowning in the ocean or standing in the middle of a freeway, stuck between racing cars.

Other nights I'd simply hear her voice. I'd hear her laugh and kiss another man. And the fear that drove me awake was not that she was in danger. The fear was that I'd lost her to someone else.

For too long, I'd ignored it and hidden in work or travel or relocating to new cities. For a time, I'd been busy caring for my mother, who never had woken up from her coma.

I'd gone to visit her in hospice nearly every day, speaking to the shell she'd once been.

No matter the current focus of my life, I'd kept Clara's memory tucked into the quiet corners of my heart.

"Nothing happened," I promised Holly.

The problem was that I wanted it to happen. I wanted Clara. No amount of time or distance would change those feelings. And Lou's words had confirmed it all. With every sentence, I'd known the right choice. He'd entrusted Hope's rings to my care, and they belonged to Clara.

Holly deserved the truth.

After I'd left Clara's room, I'd called Holly and told her I was coming home. I'd asked her to wait up. Maybe she'd heard the breakup in my voice because when I'd come through the door, she'd been in the living room. Her backpack had been beside the door, closed and full. I suspected that the toothbrush she'd left here and the extra clothes were inside.

"I'm sorry, Holly."

She sniffled and swallowed hard. "Is there anything I could have done?"

Christ, I hated this. I hated seeing hurt on her beautiful face, but she deserved to find the man who saw her and only her. "No."

"Ouch. I thought . . . I thought we had a chance."

I opened my mouth to apologize again, but she was already gone, standing from the couch and hurrying across the living room.

I followed, standing by as she picked up her backpack and purse. Then she closed the distance between us, raised up on her toes to kiss my cheek. "Goodbye, Karson."

"Goodbye, Holly."

She slipped out of the door without a backward glance.

I didn't move until the lights from her headlights had vanished. Then I bolted for the door myself, flinging it open and whipping it closed behind me as I ran for the Cadillac.

The roads to Temecula were nearly deserted as I raced to my Clara.

The hotel lobby was empty and dark. The front desk clerk side-eyed me as I jogged through the lobby for the elevator. The slow ride to our floor was torture.

It had been over three hours since I'd bid Clara good night. Was she still awake? I checked the time on my phone as I strode down the hallway toward her room. It was after midnight. She was probably asleep behind that closed door, but there was no way I was waiting until morning. "Fuck it."

I knocked lightly, waiting. If she didn't answer, I'd call. I shifted from one foot to the other, my breath lodged in my chest.

Then there was a click and the slide of a chain. Clara opened the door, wearing a pale pink silk camisole and matching sleep shorts with a lace hem. Her hair was loose, draped over her bare shoulders. But she hadn't been sleeping. There was red rimming her eyes and her cheeks were splotchy.

She'd been crying.

Lou's words clicked into place.

One look at her and the world made sense.

"I love you."

Clara gasped, her body tensing. "W-what?"

Smooth, Karson. I hadn't meant to just blurt those three words but now that they were out there, I might as well just go with it. "I love you."

She blinked, clearly confused. "What about Holly?"

"I just got back from Elyria."

"Oh." Her eyes widened. "Why?"

Why? My stomach dropped. Had I read this wrong? Did she not feel the same? *No.* No goddamn way. "Because she wasn't you."

Her chin began to quiver. "You love me?"

"I—"

"I love you too." The moment she spoke, she dropped her face into her hands. Her shoulders began to shake and I crossed the distance between us, urging her into the room before easing the door closed.

Why was she crying?

"Clara, I—"

Before I could finish my sentence, she surged, throwing her arms around my shoulders. Then there was no more talking. Her lips found mine and a bolt of lightning shot through my body, fusing me to her. We were a mess of fumbling hands and wet lips.

The urgency of her mouth. The desperation of mine. She opened for me and I dove in, my tongue tangling with hers as my arms engulfed her.

Never in my life had a kiss meant so much. I gave in, surrendering to this woman's soft lips and the slick of her tongue against mine. She clung to me as I clung to her, the softness of her body pressed into my hard lines.

This was her. This was my Clara.

And I'd kiss her every day for the rest of my life.

I scooped her up so her toes were dangling above the carpet, then I walked us to her bedroom, laying her on the bed. Covering her with my body.

Her hands came to my face, holding me to her lips, as my hands roamed down the silk of her top and shorts to the bare skin of her legs. I kneaded the flesh of her toned thighs. I drew my fingers along the back of her knee in a featherlight touch.

When she began to tremble, I forced myself to break away, going to the door and closing it quietly before flipping the lock. The sight that greeted me on the bed when I turned sent all my blood rushing to my groin.

Clara was seated on the edge of the bed. The lust in her eyes darkened them to chocolate pools. The faint light from the street outside seeped through the sheer curtains, acting like moonlight on her flawless skin.

She reached for the hem of her shirt, slowly gathering

it in her hands. Then she dragged it over her head, tossing it to the floor.

My mouth went dry. Her rosy nipples were peaked and the desperation to feel them under my palms sent me flying across the room, dropping to my knees before her.

"You are beautiful. So fucking beautiful." I slid my hands up her ribs, savoring the moan that escaped her lips. Then I found her breasts in my palms, letting them fill my hands as I raked my thumbs over her nipples.

Clara's back arched, pressing herself further into my touch. The silk of her skin was intoxicating, and tonight, I'd touch every inch. I'd lick and worship because she was mine.

"Say it again," I said, urging her down to the mattress. When that hair was splayed beneath her, I ran my hands down the swell of her hips, hooking my fingers into the shorts and the panties beneath. Then I pulled them from her legs, inch by torturous inch.

Her breath hitched when they landed on the floor. She lay bare and perfect, her gaze locked on mine.

I swallowed a groan. "Say it again."

"I love you."

"One more time."

The corner of her mouth turned up as she pushed up on her elbows, moving backward until she reached the pillows. Then she crooked a finger, beckoning me to the bed. Did she have any idea the power she had over me?

I reached behind me to yank my T-shirt over my head.

My flip-flops crashed to the carpet as Clara's gaze dropped down my stomach to the hem of my jeans. I flipped open the button, then dragged down the zipper. I shoved the pants and my black boxer briefs over my thighs, my erection bobbing free. Then I wrapped a fist around my shaft.

Clara watched as I gave it a long stroke, her eyes glued to my cock. Her cheeks were pink, her breaths heavy. "Karson."

I stayed at the foot of the bed.

"I don't have a condom." It was a fucking shame because what I wanted most was to sink inside her. To forget where I started and she began. But I'd make her come tonight, with my fingers and my tongue. "I've always used one. Always."

"I, um... not since Devan."

Fuck me. I didn't like that son of a bitch's name anywhere near a naked Clara, but knowing that she'd been without a man since was a damn rush because I'd be the last lover in her life.

"You sure?"

"I don't want to wait." She gave me a sheepish smile. "But I'm not on birth control."

Fuck, but she was shredding me here. "Your call, baby."

"I don't want to wait."

I crawled to her, hovering above her body. The intensity of her gaze was nearly my undoing as her hips cradled mine and my cock rested against her center.

"I want you to have my kids." Apparently, I had no filter tonight. Confession after confession streamed out.

Her eyes flared.

"I'm not going to hold back. I'm not going to take this slow. I've missed too many years with you, and I am not going to waste another second. You're mine. August is mine."

Her hand came to my cheek as another wash of tears flooded her eyes. There was so much emotion there. Regret for the missed years. Hope for the future.

What she felt, I felt too.

"Karson..."

"I know." I dropped a soft kiss to her mouth, running my tongue over the bottom swell of her parted lips. I deepened the kiss, treasuring her sweet taste and the feel of her bare chest against my own as I nudged against her center.

Clara locked her eyes with mine, her hands trailing down my spine toward my ass. Then I inched forward, catching her mewl with another kiss.

I rocked us together, deliberately, until I was rooted deep. "You feel so fucking good."

"Move." She hummed and locked her legs around my hips, shifting me deeper.

Ruined. I was ruined. And I relished every damn second of it.

I eased out and slid back inside her tight, wet heat. Over and over, I brought us together as her hips moved to match my rhythm. We were hushed whispers and swallowed moans. We were lost lovers making up for missed days and nights.

By the time her eyes drifted shut and her inner walls fluttered around me, the build in my lower spine was punishing. The pressure to pour myself into her was almost impossible to keep at bay.

Clara's back arched, her entire body shuddering as she held back a cry and pulsed around me. She came so hard, so strong, that I went over with her, letting the stars break across my vision and succumbing to my release.

We panted, holding tight to each other's sweaty bodies, until finally I eased away and rolled her atop my chest.

Our breaths mingled. Her ear was pressed against my heart.

"Wow."

"Holy fucking shit."

She giggled and propped her chin on my pec. "How long?"

"How long for what?"

She gave me a wicked grin. "How long until we can go again?"

I flipped her in a flash, so she was on her stomach. Then I dropped a trail of kisses over her shoulders, reaching between her legs and finding her swollen clit.

She gasped. "Already?"

"For you?" I moved up, using my free hand to pull her

hair away from her face. Then I whispered in her ear. "Always."

"SO ARE you going to be my dad?" August had never looked so serious. Gone was the boy. Instead, I was crouched beside a warrior.

A warrior who'd spend his entire life looking out for his mother.

From now on, he'd have company on the battlefield.

"I'd like to be your dad. If that's okay with you."

He looked to the sand beneath his bare feet. He squished some between his toes, then he looked over to where Clara was seated on a large blanket.

She caught his gaze and waved with one hand while the other held her phone to an ear. When we'd gotten to the beach, I'd taken August to the water while she'd called to check in with Aria.

Clara looked magnificent under the sun and on the sand. She was wearing a simple teal bikini, sexy and tempting as hell. When she'd walked out of the bedroom this morning wearing it and a sheer coverup, I'd almost lost my damn head.

It had been two days since Temecula, and I'd done exactly as I'd promised.

I hadn't gone slow.

I hadn't held back.

We'd returned to Elyria and there'd been no hotel. I'd brought Clara to my home and set her and August up in the guest bedroom.

She snuck into my room after he fell asleep each night and we spent the midnight hours exploring each other's bodies. With her by my side, I'd slept better than I had in years. So much so that when my alarm had gone off at five this morning, I'd been totally dead to the world.

If she thought I was sleeping without her again, she was dreaming.

During the day and when August was in the room, I pulled Clara in for a hug. For a kiss. Gus had been watching. Closely. Clara had sat him down for a one-on-one, but it hadn't erased all of the wariness in his gaze.

We just needed time. Thankfully, we had it.

Clara had called Aria on the way back to Elyria and told her about us. There hadn't been a lot of surprise in Aria's voice. Just a smile as she'd talked to us both on speaker.

I wondered about you two back then.

Then Aria had laughed and handed the phone to Brody.

The great thing about a boss slash brother-in-law who owned a private plane was that Clara had no pressure to rush home to Arizona. Which was good because we had some details to figure out first.

"I don't have a dad," August whispered.

There was such longing in his voice I nearly toppled

over on my ass. Kids his age started to know what made them different. For August, it was that other kids had two parents. Clara was the best mother in the world, but her days of walking alone were over.

"You do now." I put my hand on his shoulder and the smile that played on his mouth stole my heart. "I'm going to need your help."

"With what?"

I winked. "We need to find two sticks."

The light in his eyes was so much like Clara's that when I stood, I couldn't help but drop a kiss to the top of his head.

When I glanced over, Clara was watching with a hand pressed to her heart.

I waved and mouthed, "I love you."

She blew me a kiss and went back to her call.

Then August and I went exploring for our sticks. By the time we were done with our job, I went to Clara, leaving Gus to splash on the surf with his promise not to go past his knees.

"Hi." I collapsed on the blanket beside her and kissed her shoulder.

"Hi." She leaned into me. "What were you guys doing?"

"Just playing," I lied. "How's Aria?"

"Good. She asked me if I was moving here."

"Do you want to move here?" I took her hand and laced our fingers together.

"I don't know." She sighed. "I love Welcome. But I like it here too and your job is here."

"My job is flexible, baby. How's the real estate market in Welcome?"

"Probably not as exciting as it is in California." She ran her fingers through my hair. "You'd move? Really?"

"I got an email from that developer in Temecula this morning."

She sat up straighter. "And?"

"Sold. Half a million bucks, which is more than the land is worth, but he thinks there's value in the parts. So I figure that sale plus the equity I have in my house here should be plenty to set us up wherever you want to live."

"I have a house but it's on Brody and Aria's property. I love them both, but I want our own space."

"Same here." I wanted a home we chose together, where we could raise Gus and any other kids who came along.

"Do I have to decide today?"

"Yes."

She looked at me, startled for a moment, until she realized I was teasing and burst out laughing.

My God, she was beautiful when she laughed. I lunged for her, tackling her to the towel and pinning her down with a leg. Then I took her hands, raising them above her head so she was completely at my mercy. "I love you."

"I have an idea."

"What's that?"

"Let's go to your place. Give August his Nintendo and we can take a shower."

I swelled instantly, pressing the bulge against her hip. "Good idea."

She lifted her head, her lips seeking mine, but as fast as I'd pinned her, I was on my feet, bringing her with me.

"Can't leave yet."

"Why?"

I put two fingers to my lips and whistled.

August heard it, his head snapping up from where he'd been beside the water. Then he tore off, running for the spot where we'd prepared our surprise.

"Come on." I took Clara's hand, threading our fingers together, and willed my heart not to explode.

We caught up to August, who stood proudly by our creation.

"What's—" Clara's breath hitched when she saw the words we'd written in the sand. From the towel, she had been too far away to read them, but not so far that others on the beach might have ruined them.

I stepped in front of her and dropped to a knee. Then I fished the ring Lou had given me out of my shorts pocket and slid it onto her finger. "Marry me."

The words etched in the sand said the same.

Clara wouldn't have been the woman she was if her gaze hadn't shifted away from mine to August.

Behind me, August had a beaming smile on his face as he nodded.

"Yes." She crashed to her knees and framed my face with her hands.

I kissed her, lingering long enough to elicit an *eww* from August. Then I tackled Clara to the sand, getting her good and dirty as she laughed, before carrying her into the ocean and dunking us both in the water.

Needed to justify that shower.

Later that night, after we'd celebrated and decided that I had yet another move to make—we were starting our next chapter in Welcome—I found Clara at the living room window, staring at the Cadillac in the driveway.

"I'll always be grateful for that car," she whispered, then raised her hand to look at the ring. "This was his wife's, right?"

"Yeah. That was Hope's ring."

"Hope." She leaned into my chest as I wrapped her in my arms. "I like that name."

―――――

WHEN OUR DAUGHTER was born nine months later, we named her Hope.

Two years after that, we named our son Lou.

It didn't take me long to realize that no amount of exploring the world would ever be as thrilling as the adventure of living life by Clara's side.

She was the soul on earth I was made to find.

EPILOGUE
CLARA

Twenty-three years later . . .

"Have you ever seen so many stars?" I whispered.

It was like someone had shattered a diamond on a blanket of the deepest blue velvet. The white whisps and swirls of the Milky Way streaked between them like dust.

This wasn't our first trip to Montana, but the clear mountain nights never failed to take my breath away.

Karson circled his arms around me, pulling me closer as I snuggled on his lap with my eyes to the sky. "It's something, isn't it?"

"Maybe we should move to Montana."

Aria laughed from her camp chair beside ours and shared a smirk with Brody at her side. "You wouldn't make it one winter."

"True." I laughed with her, tearing my eyes from the heavens.

We were circled around a bonfire, the light from the flames flickering over familiar faces.

Londyn and Brooks.

Gemma and Easton.

Katherine and Cash.

Aria and Brody.

Me and Karson.

My friends. My family.

"When we were in high school, we'd come out here to party," Cash said, tossing another log on the bonfire before he settled into his chair beside Katherine's. "Sneak beer and girls onto the ranch."

"Ugly girls, right?" Kat asked.

"Friends. Just friends." Cash leaned over to brush a kiss to her mouth.

"And I'm sure our parents knew we were out here, just like we knew every time the kids thought they were fooling us." Easton chuckled. "Jake built a fire so big one time his senior year we could see it from the house miles away."

Gemma smiled from her husband's lap, because like me, I'd opted for a warm embrace instead of a chair of my own. "When I told him we were coming to his party spot tonight, you should have seen the look on his face. Even though he's an adult, it's fun to remind him every now and then that his mother wasn't oblivious during his teenage years."

Their son was the spitting image of Easton. Jake had grown into a tall, strong man much like his father. Their daughter, on the other hand, looked a lot like Gemma. Hailey was beautiful, elegant and witty.

Lou had a massive crush on her, something he tried so hard to hide. But my youngest son hadn't yet realized that *his* mother wasn't oblivious either.

"Ellie's boyfriend seems nice," I told Londyn.

Brooks grumbled. "He's too nice. I don't trust him."

Londyn rolled her eyes. "*Someone* is having a hard time accepting that his three children are no longer children."

"Grandpa Brooks," Gemma teased. "Wyatt's twins sure are growing up fast. It feels like just yesterday they were three and we were giving them pony rides around the arena."

"It was yesterday." He chuckled. "Where is time going? When did we get old?"

"You're not the only one struggling," Brody said, sharing a look with Aria. "Trace told us on the trip up that he was offered a job in Dublin and is thinking of taking it."

"Dublin." I pressed a hand to my heart and looked to my sister. "That's an ocean away."

She shrugged, but the worry line between her eyebrows deepened. "Good thing we own an airplane."

And I doubted Millie would ever stray far from her

parents, especially now that she'd graduated from college and taken a job with Brody's company. After he'd inherited Carmichael Communications from his family, he'd sold it and made a fortune. Then he'd turned around and started another mega-successful company with Millie under his wing. She was Aria's best friend and worshiped her dad.

"Who needs another beer?" Katherine asked. Her chair was closest to the cooler we'd brought out. When hands lifted, she popped up and hurried to deliver frosty bottles. Cash put his hand on her thigh when she returned to her seat, drawing circles on her jeans with his thumb to show her his love. And to trap her in the chair.

I'd give it five minutes before she was up again, finding something else to busy herself with. Katherine was coping with her emotions through perpetual motion.

"Good thing we snagged that cooler when we did," Easton said. "All the kids were congregating at the lodge and I saw the beginning of a party starting."

That was typical. Years ago, the parties had been sleeping bags and hot cocoa and popcorn from the floor while they watched a movie projected onto a white wall. Then later, the parties had been games and teenage jokes until three in the morning. Maybe a kiss snuck here and there.

Our kids had grown up together. We lived in our own worlds and different towns, but at least once a year for the past twenty-three years, we'd come to Montana and spent a week at the Greer Ranch and Mountain Resort.

Now that our kids were out of the house, Karson and I came to Montana every few months. Arizona was home base, where we worked and lived, but the travel bug—Karson's love of exploring—had infected us both.

We went to Elyria a few times a year. We loved Hawaii and New York and London and Melbourne. Though most of our trips were to see the kids.

Hope had moved to Phoenix after graduating from college to work as a trainer for the Arizona Cardinals football franchise. Lou still had a year left at Stanford and then he was planning on law school. He'd mentioned a few schools on the East Coast, and I'd bitten my tongue before I could protest.

Like Aria had said, they owned a plane, one that they insisted Karson and I use often.

That plane had taken numerous trips to Montana, and not just for the annual summer reunion.

August had decided to go to Montana State for college, and I'd known his freshman year we'd lost him to the mountains.

Then we'd lost him to Delilah.

Not that I was complaining, because I loved her too. I'd loved her since she was a baby.

This year's trip to Montana wasn't just the yearly get-together. This year's trip was special.

In two days, August was marrying Cash and Katherine's oldest daughter.

It would be a wonderful spectacle compared to the courthouse ceremony Karson and I'd had at the Welcome courthouse, when I'd been a month pregnant with Hope.

August and Delilah's wedding promised to be a fancy affair. Hundreds of guests. A white gown. Five tiers of cake and a live band for the reception after the three-course meal.

Since we'd arrived earlier in the week, it had been nothing but wedding madness. August and Delilah were getting married in a meadow on the ranch. Cash and Easton had been working hard to get the field mowed and free of cowpies. Katherine, Gemma and the entire Greer family had spent months planning and preparing for the reception in the lodge.

It was all coming together but there had been plenty of work to do this week, leading up to the big day.

Tonight was the first time since we'd arrived that there hadn't been a planned function. It was the first time we'd gathered, just us. The runaways and our loves.

"Let's ask them now," I whispered into my husband's ear.

"Okay." He kissed my cheek.

I took a fortifying breath, then looked around our circle. "We wanted to run something by you guys."

"For the wedding?" Kat asked, sitting straighter.

"Sort of." I laced my fingers through Karson's, silently telling him to take over.

Like Katherine, I was a bundle of emotion this week. While she buried hers in activity, I'd resorted to what seemed like an endless stream of near-tear moments.

I was so happy for Gus. I was so proud of the man he'd become. And he loved Delilah with every cell in his body, treating her with such adoration and respect. I'd told him as much in another mess of tears a few days ago. Gus had hugged me and said he'd learned that from watching Karson. His dad.

But happy and proud, I still felt like I was losing my baby boy. So I'd been leaning on my husband, like tonight, to speak up for me when I couldn't get the words past the lump in my throat.

"We drove the Cadillac up here," Karson said. "As you know."

The day we'd pulled into the lodge's parking lot, everyone else had already been here. They'd descended on the car, greeting it like an old friend. This wasn't the first trip to Montana that we'd brought the car, and like past times, having it here gave everyone the chance to drive it again.

Gemma and Katherine had taken it to town on grocery store runs. Londyn and Brooks had spent a few hours getting lost on the Montana highways. Then Aria and Brody had done the same.

"We want to give it to August and Delilah," Karson said. "As a wedding present. But we wanted to check with you guys first."

The crackle of the fire was the only sound.

Then Londyn nodded and the smile that stretched across her face was brighter than the flames. "Yes. Absolutely."

"Best idea ever." Gemma nodded.

Cash shook his head in disbelief. "Are you sure?"

"It's time for that car to go to the next generation," Karson answered. "Your daughter. My son. I can't think of a better pair. And maybe someday, they'll continue the tradition. Send it down the road with someone else who needs it."

Katherine buried her face in her hands, her shoulders shaking. Cash stood and scooped her up, settling her on his lap. She took a moment, then sniffled and looked up, drying her eyes. "Sorry. I'm a wreck this week. Who needs another beer?"

Cash trapped her before she could stand. "No one needs another beer, sweetheart."

"Let's have a toast." Aria raised her beer bottle into the air. "To the original Lou."

I smiled. She'd deemed one Lou the original and the other Lou—my son—*the famous Lou*. "To the original Lou."

The circle cheered.

Lou usually got a toast at these functions. He'd stuck with us all, decades later, especially since every woman in the circle was wearing a piece of his jewelry. Lou had gifted Hope's jewelry to us all, along with our own respective letters.

Well, except for me.

Over the years, we'd shared the contents of those letters with each other. Mostly, Lou had written about his wife. Combined, those letters had given us a glimpse of his love for Hope, and wearing something of hers was an honor.

To Londyn, he'd gifted a gold locket. To Gemma, an opal pendant necklace. To Katherine, a pair of ruby stud earrings. To Aria, a ring adorned with tiny gold roses. I wore Hope's wedding rings as my own. And Karson wore Lou's wedding band, the piece Lou had gifted to me.

It was almost like he'd known that the man it was destined for was Karson. I liked to think so.

I dropped my forehead to Karson's, closing my eyes. "I love you."

"Love you too, baby." He cupped my cheek, tipping my face so he could cover my lips with his. We kissed like we had in the beginning. We kissed like we hadn't kissed for twenty-three years. We kissed like two people who had never taken our days for granted.

After I pulled my lips away from Karson's, I sat up straighter. "One more toast. To the junkyard."

It had long been demolished, but it lived in our hearts.

"To the junkyard," nine other voices said in unison.

To the place where our stories had started and the place we'd found a family.

To the place where I'd found the love of my life.

To the place that would bind us together forever.

ACKNOWLEDGMENTS

The Runaway series started as a side project—a passion project—and it stole my heart. Thank you for reading *Dotted Lines*! Thank you for reading all of these stories. I hope you've loved these junkyard kids and this Cadillac ride as much as I have.

Special thanks to my editing and proofreading team: Elizabeth, Julie, Karen and Judy. Thank you to Sarah Hansen for the cover.

A huge thanks to the members of my reader group. Your love and support truly make me smile each and every day. Thank you to the bloggers who read and promote my stories. I am so grateful for you all.

Thank you to my friends and family. And thank you to my husband and two beautiful boys for letting me escape into these fictional worlds and greet me with big smiles and big hugs when I come back to reality.

ABOUT THE AUTHOR

Devney Perry is a *Wall Street Journal*, *USA Today* and #1 Amazon bestselling author of over forty romance novels. After working in the technology industry for a decade, she abandoned conference calls and project schedules to pursue her passion for writing. She was born and raised in Montana and now lives in Washington with her husband and two sons.

Don't miss out on the latest book news.
Subscribe to her newsletter!
www.devneyperry.com

Printed in Dunstable, United Kingdom